The Spell and the Octopus

"Put me down, Thorolf!" Countess Yvette said. "I can hold my liquor."

When her feet came to the floor, she pushed Thorolf down, sat on his lap, and kissed him vigorously. "There," she said. "Now you shall learn what you should have found out years agone."

"I only hope I can meet your expectations," Thorolf said.

The countess broke off. "Thorolf, I feel very strange of a sudden!"

"After all that liquor—but then, too, it must be time for Bardi's spell to take effect," Thorolf said sententiously.

"Oh, I had forgotten! Ouch! I am in pain . . . glub . . ."

As Thorolf gazed with mounting horror, the golden-haired woman changed before his eyes. Her limbs became limp, as if their bones had dissolved. Her face lost form and sank into her body. The thing on the settee was no longer remotely human!

The octopus whipped tentacles around Thorolf's neck and hoisted its body into his lap. It pressed its beak against his bare chest, but did not bite him; it merely touched his skin lightly here and there. Thorolf realized it was trying to kiss him!

By L. Sprague de Camp
Published by Ballantine Books:

THE RELUCTANT KING
Volume One: THE GOBLIN TOWER
Volume Two: THE CLOCKS OF IRAZ
Volume Three: THE UNBEHEADED KING

THE HONORABLE BARBARIAN
LEST DARKNESS FALL
THE BEST OF L. SPRAGUE DE CAMP
THE COMPLEAT ENCHANTER
THE ANCIENT ENGINEERS

By L. Sprague & Catherine Crook de Camp
Published by Ballantine Books:

THE PIXILATED PEERESS

The Pixilated Peeress

L. Sprague de Camp and Catherine Crook de Camp

A Del Rey Book

BALLANTINE BOOKS • NEW YORK

A Del Rey Book
Published by Ballantine Books
Copyright © 1991 by L. Sprague de Camp and Catherine Crook de Camp

Library of Congress Catalog Card Number: 90-93528

ISBN 0-345-36733-2

Manufactured in the United States of America

First Hardcover Edition: August 1991
First Mass Market Edition: September 1992

Contents

Foreword

This novel is laid in the same fictitious world as *The Incorporated Knight*, but a few decades later, with different characters. The setting roughly resembles that of fifteenth-century Europe. If anyone wonders, "Rhaetia" can best be pronounced "Reesha," rhyming with "Grecia" and "magnesia."

There is, by the way, a real Green Dragon Inn in Hereford, England. When we were there in 1978 with a niece and a granddaughter, we were chased out at 6:00 A.M. in our nightclothes by a false fire alarm.

L. Sprague de Camp
Catherine Crook de Camp
Plano, Texas

I
The Captivating Countess

Thorolf Zigramson laid his scabbarded sword on the grass and baited his hook with a squirming green grub. He tossed the hook into the pool in the mountain stream and watched the crimson float bob amid the silvery ripples. He gathered his russet cloak to sit down on the greensward when, a few paces downstream, a holly-green spruce sapling spoke:

"Goodman! Pray give me some clothes!"

Thorolf started. Dropping his fishpole, he clapped a bronze hand to the hilt of his dagger. "What say you, bush?"

The sapling's voice, though musical still, took on a note of command. "I said, give me some clothes! Your cloak will do, to start."

"Forsooth! And why should I give my good Tyrrhenian mantle away to the first bush that begs for it?"

The voice grew sharp. "Cease calling me 'bush,' knave!"

"Why? Prefer you 'shrub'? Or perchance 'evergreen'?"

"Oaf! The proper address for one of my rank is 'my lady' or 'your Highness.' "

Thorolf sheathed his dagger with a smile. "A female shrub, forsooth? You are the first plant I ever heard to claim nobility. Not that it signifies aught in Rhaetia; we long ago abolished titles."

The soprano voice rose in exasperation. "I know that, yokel! That is why you have no government worth the name. But I am in sore need of garments. You should have the courtesy—"

"Come out and tell me who you be, and I'll consider."

"I cannot."

"Wherefore not?" demanded Thorolf.

"I am not decent."

Thorolf smiled through his beard. "Let not that prevent you. I know persons of all degrees, including some given to crass indecencies."

"Not indecent in a moral sense, blockhead! I beg your raiment because I lack proper attire."

With slow deliberation, Thorolf picked up his fishpole. "No meeting, no garments. Now go away; you frighten the fish."

"Incondite rascal! I'll show thee!"

From behind the conifer sapling stepped a slight, fairskinned young woman, naked save for a golden coronet on her aureate hair. Although but little over five feet tall and a jot too slender for Thorolf's taste, she was a beautiful creature.

"Good gods!" he exclaimed, dropping his rod for the second time. "Are you, mayhap, the Queen of the Fairies?"

"Nay; a mortal woman in distress. I hight Yvette, Countess of Grintz."

Thorolf glanced up uncertainly at the snowcapped peaks of the Helvetians, where dwelt the trolls; then bowed slightly. "Forsooth, Countess, your garb becomes you, albeit a trifle impractical for this cool mountain clime."

He picked up his cloak, shook a fallen leaf out of its folds, and handed it to the woman, who swirled it around herself. Since Thorolf was big, all the Countess but her coroneted head disappeared into the russet garment.

"How gat you into this predicament, my lady?" he asked.

"I fled the men of Duke Gondomar of Landai, who pursued me across the border. Thinking I had given them the slip for good, I paused for a dip in this stream, in a pool well below this one. Whilst bathing I heard their clatter round the bend of the Rissel and outcry as they espied my mount and abandoned garments. Ere they came in sight, I splashed across to the farther bank, climbed out, and ran. Seeing you, I hid behind that tree."

"Did the men of the Duke discover you?"

"Methinks not."

Thorolf considered what he might do if he were chasing such a quarry. The Duke's men plainly paid no heed to Rhaetian sovereignty. While reflecting, he changed the subject:

"Why do you wear that little crown? It suits not your bathing costume."

Unsmilingly, Yvette replied: "I dared not lay down my coronet whilst I did bathe, and a good thing, too. Lacking gold and jewels, I count upon this bauble to pay for mercenaries to regain my lands."

Aside from the Countess' beauty and unconventional garb, Thorolf was struck by the woman's utter self-confidence. So certain an aristocratic poise aroused in him—a Commonwealth citizen owing no devoir to any noble—a shadowy urge to kneel and utter oaths of fealty. He conquered the impulse but reflected that the sage who proclaimed that universal nudity would place

3

all mankind on a uniform level had never met Yvette of Grintz. To cover his momentary confusion he gruffly said:

"That cloak is but a loan, my lady. I shall want it back when we find you more suitable raiment."

Yvette studied him. "Trust a Rhaetian to keep close track of's property! But from your speech you are no yokel. Who in sooth are you?"

Thorolf placed a hand on his chest and bowed. "Acting Sergeant Thorolf Zigramson of the Fourth Commonwealth Foot, at your service."

"Oh, a soldier! You have the thews for it." She studied the massively muscled, broad-shouldered young man from his short black hair and well-trimmed beard to his dusty, well-worn boots. "Findst it an exciting trade?"

He considered. "Not the word I'd use, madam. True, just before a battle one's heart beats faster, when one is torn betwixt fear of what's coming and fear of showing one's fear. When the fighting starts, one is too busy trying to save one's life whilst depriving others of theirs to think on such matters. But most of a soldier's time is plain hard work, especially since we adopted the Batavian system."

"What's that?"

"All men of a unit must dress exactly alike. When my father served his hitch as a youth, to tie a colored scarf about one's arm or hat sufficed; but no more. If, however, a garment gives out on a campaign, the soldier must buy or steal whatever replacement he can. So an army that sets forth brave in uniform garb returns in motley.

"Then we must drill, drill, drill, so that all shall obey instantly and precisely, as if the soldier were but a cogwheel in a vast machine of clockwork."

"Ugh!" she said. "It sounds dreadfully dull."

"It is, but it works. Thus the Batavians drove the Emperor's troops from their swampy land."

4

She changed the subject. "Said you Thorolf Zigramson?"

"Aye."

"Then, are you perchance kin to Consul Zigram?"

"My father."

As Yvette began another question, Thorolf raised a hand. "Let's intermit the questions, Countess. If we stand here havering, your Duke's men may yet catch us in their dip net. Shog along!"

Thorolf hoisted his baldric over his head and gathered pole, net, and creel.

Yvette said: "I cannot walk far; my poor feet are half flayed."

"My horse is nigh. She'll bear the twain."

When they reached the big, staked-out mare, Yvette frowned. "This cloak were of small avail for riding pillion. Couldst lend me your hosen?"

Thorolf sighed. "Your Ladyship is not the easiest damsel to succor; I fancy riding bare-arsed no more than you. But—here!" He peeled off his leather jacket and then his white linen shirt. The latter he held out, saying, "Put your legs in the sleeves and tie the shirttails about your waist."

With a sputter of laughter, Yvette complied. Thorolf looked her over. "Unsuitable for a coronation ball; but 'twill do, 'twill suffice. Now place your foot in my hands, and up you go!"

They trotted briskly along a little-used trail, with Yvette, clutching Thorolf's belt and hiding her coronet within the cloak, perched sideways on the horse's rump. The path sloped down. As they reached the lower levels, deciduous trees—oak, beech, and maple—appeared among the ubiquitous conifers, their foliage crisp and brown with the fading of summer. Over his shoulder, the soldier remarked:

"Now, what was that you said when first we met, about our democratic government?"

Yvette responded crisply: "It is a standing invitation to mob rule and anarchy."

"I beg to differ," drawled Thorolf. "Our public men may not all be saints or heroes, but we've never elected a consul like that ass, King Valdhelm the Third of Locania, who betimes imagines himself a watering pot and wanders his palace pissing on potted plants."

"Indeed, and what of the Rhaetian Consul who made off with half your treasury when he fled the land?"

"True," said Thorolf equably. "But if an official of ours do prove a fool or a knave, we cast him out at the next election. The Locanians have no voice in choosing their rulers, as all us Rhaetians do."

"All but your women," said Yvette acidly. "Aha, that punctured your self-satisfaction!"

"Well, ah," said Thorolf, "the general opinion is that women be not equally endowed in such matters."

"Thinkst not I be as able a politician as the best of your men? I work as hard for my people's welfare as do any of your senators or consuls. But in your land every Rhaetian with pintle and stones in's crotch may vote, be he as dumb as an ox, whilst the ablest woman is barred. Why not give male trolls the vote?"

Thorolf raised a quizzical eyebrow. "Trolls are not deemed human. If we start down through the animal kingdom, as well extend the franchise to bulls and billy goats."

"Trolls are human enough to beget offspring on human women and to burrow for ores to make your nails and swords!"

"True, but trolls are still not citizens. When my sire was senator, he proposed defining them as human, thus entitling them to the law's protection; but the others took it as a jest."

"You evade the point, Master Thorolf. A folk cannot thrive without stability, and that requires a framework of hereditary lordships."

"And what stability, forsooth, has your feudalism given the Grintzers?"

"Enough of this subject, Sergeant! How come you to ride a mare? Methought men of valor eschewed them, lest they be infected by womanish qualities—or those traits they falsely attribute to my sex."

Thorolf chuckled. "Mere superstition. Salnia's as brave amongst horses as you are amongst women. And she takes me whither I would go."

"Rhaetian practicality!" said the Countess with a trace of a sneer. "Are you never chaffed about her?"

"One of my men jibed me. I picked him up by the ankles and dipped his head in a rain barrel until he agreed to hold his tongue."

"Fear not that I shall ever taunt you, at least if there be a rain barrel nigh! But how came you, with your connections and learning, to this lowly rank?"

"Not so lowly, madam. I am responsible for the welfare and conduct of a hundred men—or should be were my company up to strength." After a pause he added: "When I returned from my studies abroad, seeking an academic career, I obtained a readership at Horgus College."

"What transmogrified you from apprentice professor to soldier?"

"A trifle of trouble," said Thorolf uneasily, sorry that he had brought the subject up.

"What trouble?"

" 'Tis a flat, weary, and unprofitable tale."

At Thorolf's hint of reticence, Yvette came alert, like a cat that espies a dilatory mouse. "Tell me natheless!" she said in tones of queenly command.

"If you insist. When the Franconians conquered the Duchy of Dorelia, a crowd of students burst into my classroom, demanding that I sign a manifesto on behalf of freedom for the Dorelians. I refused."

"Wherefore?"

"I said that, first, this was a class in Tyrrhenian lit-

7

erature and not a political forum; second, that my signature would do nought to loosen King Chilperic's grip on the land; and finally, that it mattered little to the Dorelian masses whether they were fleeced by a duke or a king.''

"What's this about people being 'fleeced' by their natural lords? In my country . . .''

"Hush!'' Thorolf drew rein and, turning his head, held a finger to his lips.

"But—'' began Yvette.

"Quiet! Not a word!'' snapped Thorolf. "I listen for pursuers.''

Yvette subsided, scowling. When Thorolf was satisfied he could hear no jingle of arms or creak of harness, he clucked the mare into motion.

"Insolent upstart!'' shrilled Yvette. "Thus to order about a peeress born! In Grintz you'd be flogged till the skin of your back—''

"But this is not Grintz, and you have no bullies to jump to your commands. If you give trouble, I'll set you down instanter, and without my borrowed garments. Is that your wish, Countess?''

Yvette silently fumed, her breath sibilating through clenched white teeth. Far above, the scarlet sunlight lingered on a snow-crested peak, then slowly shrank and faded. The only sound was the patient footfalls of the burdened mare.

At last Yvette muttered a few words that Thorolf took for a grudging apology. She asked: "What did the students next?''

"One emptied a slop pail over my head.''

"And then?''

"I threw him out the window and asked if others would care to follow him. None volunteered, hearing the yells of him who'd broken a leg in's fall. His family went to law and won a thousand-mark judgment against the college. And away went my professorial plans.''

"So you became a soldier?"

"Indeed. My father said: 'With those shoulders, and having no talent for commerce or finance, 'tis the army for you, my lad.' "

Yvette exclaimed: "But every Rhaetian's born with a ledger in his fist; else he's like a fish that cannot swim." After a pause, she added: "Hast fought in a battle?"

"A small affray with revolutionaries from Tzenric. They promised to abolish taxes and give every Rhaetian a stipend, so that none need ever work again."

Yvette tightened her grasp on Thorolf's belt and shook her head. "Just the sort of mountebanks your democratic fools might elect! Didst cross blades with those joltheads?"

"I made a few hits; but in such a brabble none knows for certain who does what to whom. In truth, I cared but little for the outcome. I'm a peaceable wight who'd liefer spend his days in scholarship.

"Now tell me of your plans anent the Duke. That coronet should fetch a few thousand, but such a purse would not long survive an assault upon a dukedom."

Yvette chewed her lip. "I could doubtless raise a good few thousand more within a year—"

Thorolf interrupted: "Still insufficient, I fear. Since King Chilperic has hired away our likeliest bullies for his Dorelian war, the pay of mercenaries has risen. My company is down to eighty-odd, since lusty youths earn more as camp cooks and stablemen."

Yvette sniffed. "Trust Rhaetians to value money above honor!"

Thorolf chuckled. "As says the buffoon in one of Helmanax's plays: 'Who hath honor? He that was buried yesterday.' "

"Might I not engage your Rhaetian regulars?"

"Nay; the Consul has forbidden the hiring thereof for foreign adventures."

* * *

For half an hour, only the chirps of birds, the hum of insects, and the horse's hoofbeats broke the silence of the descending road. At last Yvette spoke:

"Then I must needs seek magical help. I hear that the King of Locania, since he got the religious bee in's bonnet, hath exiled all his magicians. Many have found a haven in Rhaetia."

"True," admitted Thorolf.

"How about Doctor Orlandus, the great Psychomagus?"

"He advances grandiose claims, but I trust him no more than I trust the ice on Lake Zurshnitt in spring. Some dub him one part wizard and three parts charlatan."

"They say he doth command those spirits called deltas."

Thorolf shrugged. "I know nought of that. I do know howsomever an able iatromage, Doctor Bardi. He waxes old and infirm but retains enough prowess to banish the colds in my head.

"And, Countess, if it be not unmeet to ask, should not your husband, the Count of Grintz, and his retainers defend your county?"

"I am the late Count's widow. As a woman without issue, I am by law sole ruler until I wed again."

"What befell the Count? Battle or a tisick?"

"Neither. Count Volk had seen his eightieth winter when my sire, the Baron Grombac, betrothed me to him, thinking it a brilliant match. On our wedding night, this dotard braced himself and actually sheathed his blade ere his poor old heart gave up."

"Monstrous awkward for you!" exclaimed Thorolf.

"Awkward indeed!" Yvette shuddered. "I, a slender lass of scarce sixteen, had to roll that great carcass . . . Howsomever, that is the reason I am acting Countess."

"How gat you into Duke Gondomar's bad book?"

"A few years after Volk died in vain pursuit of his youth, my sire, upon his deathbed, promised me to Gondomar. But I, misliking the arrogant brute, threw his marriage contract in his face and refused to wed him. After my father's funeral, Gondomar came back with his army, vowing to bed me with or without the Divine Pair's blessing.

"I let it be known that I'd slay any man who sought to futter me against my will, if it meant stabbing him in his sleep. I beat off his first attempt, and for years I lived behind my castle walls, like a captive or cloistered nun. Last month the Duke returned and this time prevailed."

"Strange that a lady of your qualities and demesne did not find a hundred would-be spouses rattling her castle gates!"

"Oh, I've had offers aplenty, but none that suited," Yvette replied disdainfully. "My next husband must be, imprimus, of noble rank; secundus, a shrewd and mettlesome man of affairs, able at running the county; and tertius, a poet who can ensorcel me with romantical fancies. And, it goes without saying, a strong-loined lover and a man who will heed my advice in county matters."

Thorolf whistled. "Even one of our pagan gods were hard-pressed to meet your requirements! Certes I could not, though I used to compose a few versicles. But one cannot live on poetry in Rhaetia, where merchants and bankers rule."

"You a poet? Ha, can your horse play the lute? 'Twere no more credible. Pray give an ensample!"

"Let me think." While he pondered, the chirp of birds dwindled to silence with the fading of light. A cricket struck up its shrill song, while overhead an early flittermouse whirred. At last Thorolf spoke:

"My lady, the mistress of Castle Contentious,
Is hunting a husband of standing pretentious;
But I, a plain wight of opinions sententious,
Am loath to embark on a lifetime dissentious!"

"Ouch!" he exclaimed as Yvette boxed his right ear. "What's that for?"

"Insolent malapert! You, a commoner, jesting that had I the absurdity to offer you my hand, you'd have the effrontery to reject my proposal! Had you voiced such a thought in my demesne—"

"But we are not in your demesne. And if you seek to treat me as one of your serfs, you may wend afoot for all I care."

Yvette subsided, though Thorolf caught a murmur that resembled the expletives of a fishmonger who found he had taken counterfeit coins for his wares. As they rode on in silence, the soldier began to suspect that despite her notable virtues, the Countess was lacking in humor. He wondered what had happened to the knights in the old romances and the ladies fair who decked them with silken scarves and meekly awaited their return from adventures. Meekness was certainly not the style of Yvette of Grintz.

At last she spoke again, in normal tones: "Pray understand, good my soldier, that I could never entertain a proposal of marriage from one of your class. The fact that you have worked for wages debars you forever from alliance with one of noble blood."

Thorolf raised an eyebrow. "What is so demeaning about earning an honest living?"

"That you do so doth you credit; but a noble must devote all his strength to the welfare of those whom the Divine Pair have placed beneath his rule, leaving no time to toil for gain. He must strain at the practice of arms each day, whilst his lady spends her waking hours in the conduct of their establishment. Knowst the tale of Count Helfram of Trongai?"

"What befell him?"

"As a result of untimely misfortunes, he found himself unable to pay his servants to man the castle. Indeed, he could not even buy sufficient food to feed his family. So he donned a bogus beard, went to town, and persuaded the local taverner to hire him as bartender.

"All went well until one day a drunken customer, seeking a quarrel, remarked on the barkeep's piggy eyes and other features that the fellow deemed obnoxious. Count Helfram, unused to insolence, slapped the man's face, whereupon the drunkard seized the false beard and tore it off.

"The other folk recognized their Count and rose as one to hurl the drunkard into the street. But the tale took wings, until the King of Carinthia, hearing the rumor, ruled that Helfram had forfeited his rank, and the king appointed a new Count from another branch of the family. The last I heard, poor Helfram was still tending bar at the tavern, whither people came from afar to gape at a nobleman toiling like a commoner."

"Then," said Thorolf cheerfully, "I count myself lucky to have no noble rank to lose. We must hasten, for the dragon wing of night o'erspreads the earth, as saith the man in Helmanax's play."

He heeled his horse to stir the beast to further effort. After they had ridden in silence for a time, Yvette continued:

"At all events, I would never marry a Rhaetian. You're an unromantic lot, whose only knights are those little tin figurines that pop out of your clocks to mark the hours. None could essay the doughty deeds of romances."

Thorolf laughed. "Suppose a knight engaged in such deeds in this modern world! If he slew a dragon, he'd be arrested by the game warden for hunting out of season, as I believe once truly befell a Locanian knight in Pathenia, not long ago. If he snatched a maiden from an enchanter vile, the mage would hale him to law on charges of abduction. If he even sang a roundelay beneath his true love's casement window, the song's composer would demand a royalty."

"A typical Rhaetian argument," retorted Yvette,

"mired in base practicality! A sorry world we live in!" After a pause she asked: "For what goal, pray, do you strive?"

Thorolf frowned thoughtfully. "To settle, once and for all, the authorship of the Tyrrhenian play, *Il Bastimento dai Pazzi*, doubtfully attributed to Goldinú."

"You would waste your life in thumbing dusty manuscripts to settle some obscure pedantic dispute?"

Thorolf shrugged. "To me it's more fun than standing daily in the drill yard and bawling at my company: 'About—face! Forward—march! Hartmund, get in step!' "

"Either were better than turning brigand, I ween," she said. "But this merely reinforces my point: that you are a typical stolid, avaricious, unromantic Rhaetian. As a noblewoman's consort, you'd be as out of place as a pig in a horse race."

"Avaricious?" Thorolf gave his most irritating chuckle. "My sire complains that I be not mercenary enough. And whilst we're trading flatteries, as a wife you'd be as useful to a soldier as slippers to a serpent. I fear, my dear Countess, you'll search the wide world over without finding your notion of a suitable spouse."

Yvette sighed. "Whilst I loathe to concede a point, you may be right. Many I've seen with one or another of my qualifications, but never one who met all. Methought I'd found my mate in a handsome troubadour who boasted blue blood and showed a promising grasp of county management; but he soon moved on."

"The scurvy lown!" said Thorolf suppressing a grin. He felt he understood the troubadour.

"Pray, treat all I've said as secret. I should not have so confided in a stranger, and a commoner at that; but my sire did ever chide me on my runaway tongue."

"Your secrets are safe with me. And now good news." He pointed ahead. "Yonder lies Vulfilac's smithy, around the bend."

* * *

The mare picked up her ears, as if sensing the journey's end, and trotted smartly over the remaining distance. She drew up before a pair of doors that led into the forge.

Thorolf dismounted and lifted Yvette off. She stood disheveled, clutching Thorolf's cloak around herself and the coronet.

"Wait here," he said. "I would not startle Vulfilac by your unforewarned appearance."

Thorolf strode into the smithy, where the firelight danced to the beat of hammered metal, while sparks flew out the open portal into the night like fugitive crimson fireflies. Inside the doors, a vestibule led to the smith's small dwelling, huddled against the much larger workplace.

"Aha, Sergeant Thorolf!" boomed the giant smith. "Glad to see you am I!" He continued to pound a bar of red-hot iron, which he held on the anvil by tongs. Setting hammer and tongs aside, he called to the boy who was pumping the bellows: "Take a rest, son. We have a visitor."

"Two visitors," said Thorolf, embracing his gigantic friend despite the smith's sooty face and forearms. Presently the two men came out and hastened toward Yvette. Thorolf said: "Countess, I present my trusted friend Vulfilac Smith. He has some clothes for you."

The smith bowed as Yvette smiled, saying: "Your health, goodman! Where are these garments?"

"In my poor house, your Highness. Will ye step thither?"

In the smithy, they passed a great rack of tools: tongs, files, and hammers with heads of various shapes, round, pointed, and wedged. Unlatching a small door, the smith led his guests into the common room of his dwelling. He unlocked an ancient armoire, mumbling:

"I've kept my goodwife's things for sentiment; but ye are welcome to any or all, my lady."

Smiling, Yvette approached the wardrobe and, still

clutching her coronet beneath the cloak, began to rummage. Studying a bodice, she said:

"Methinks your late wife was fuller of breast than I."

"Aye, and taller, too, the gods preserve her soul."

"Amen," said Yvette. "Had she hosen and shoon?"

"Aye." The smith opened drawers beneath the cupboards.

"Splendid!" said Yvette, rummaging anew. "Goodman, your generosity shall be well repaid when I obtain the wherewithal. Meanwhile my thanks must suffice."

The smith gazed at the little countess with the awe of one who beheld Rianna, the goddess of love. "If—if your Highness mind not our simple rustic fare . . ."

"You offer to dine us? Mind? I embrace your offer; hungry as I am, your simplest repast were a banquet. Now I beg your leave, good people, to dress."

The men withdrew, the smith to the cookhouse, Thorolf to stable and feed his horse.

When Thorolf returned, Vulfilac was ladling stew into bowls while his son carved a loaf of black bread into slices. Yvette waited, clad as the complete goodwife, with a flounced petticoat showing below her skirt. Below the petticoat were red wool stockings and stout leather sollerets. On her head was a barillet, a miniature turban held in place by a wimple beneath her chin. Handing Thorolf his cloak and shirt, she spoke:

"Friends, the stars do shine and I do starve. Let the feast begin!"

The repast was nearly done when Yvette held up the coronet. "Goodman Vulfilac, canst find me an old cloth wherein to wrap this thing? It were folly to flaunt it in town."

"Aye," said the smith. "Son, attend to the matter." Waving his spoon, he continued the talk of his trade: "As I was saying, it takes a sharp judgment to tell the heat of iron by its color. Ye start hammering when it glows a buttercup yellow and keep on till it cools to dark red. If ye smite it thereafter, 'tis labor wasted. But if ye heat it up to white, so that it shoots out sparkles, then ye've overheated the piece and spoilt it. It were good for nought but scrap, to be melted up again. . . ." The smith turned toward the door. "What's that?"

Outside, horsemen were dismounting. "Gondomar's men!" Yvette exclaimed. "What shall I do?"

"Out the scullery door, quick!" snapped Thorolf. "Hide in the woods. Hold the forge door with me, Vulfilac."

"Show her the way, lad!" said Vulfilac. The boy gathered up the bundle he had made of the coronet. He and the Countess fled hand in hand. The shouts and hammering grew more insistent as Thorolf picked up his sword and followed Vulfilac into the smithy, where the smith chose four heavy hammers off the wall.

They reached the open door to be confronted by five men; behind them a sixth held their horses. Four of the five grasped swords, while the fifth cradled a cocked crossbow. The leader was a heavy-set man wearing a white surcoat over his leather, metal-studded cuirass. On the chest of this garment was broidered an emblem, but the man wore his surcoat inside out so that the patch was hidden.

"Where is the Countess Yvette?" barked this man.

"We know nought of that lady," said Thorolf.

"Liar! We tracked her to the pool on the Rissel whereat ye fished, and anon a peasant saw her riding pillion behind you. Say where she be and we'll not harm you twain."

"I cannot tell you what I do not know," retorted Thorolf. "So be off with you!"

Vulfilac added: " 'Tis an unseemly time to be pounding an honest workman's door—"

"Take them!" said the leader, pointing with his sword.

The four swordsmen advanced in a semicircle; but as they closed in to pass beneath the lintel, they crowded one another. Vulfilac hurled one of his hammers. With a crunch, it struck the nearest raider in the face and threw him prone and still, his face a mask of blood.

Swords clanged and grated. Thorolf found himself hotly engaged with two of the swordsmen, one of them the leader, while the remaining swordsman danced about just beyond reach of the smith's hammers. Vulfilac made another throw, but the swordsman ducked.

"Get away and give me a clear shot!" cried the crossbowman in the rear.

Another thrown hammer caught Vulfilac's opponent in the belly and sent him reeling, doubled over and retching. One of Thorolf's two looked around for his comrade. Thorolf, till then compelled to remain on the defensive, took advantage of the pause to skewer him of the surcoat with a coupé; his blade punched through the leather corselet into the flesh beneath. The man folded up with a groan. The other swordsman found both the sergeant and the smith advancing upon him.

He ran back, while the crossbowman leveled his weapon. Without armor, Thorolf felt naked. At that range, the bolt would tear through his guts like a skewer through butter. Beside him, Vulfilac wound up to throw his last hammer.

The crossbowman backed away, swinging his weapon so that it bore first upon one antagonist and then the other. At that moment a small figure appeared in the dusk behind the arbalester. The newcomer picked up one of the thrown hammers, lofted it high, and smote the crossbowman's head from behind. The arbalester collapsed.

The raider who had been struck in the belly scuttled painfully to the horses. The unwounded swordsman and the groom who had held the animals boosted him into the saddle. Leading three riderless animals, the survivors cantered off. Holding the hammer she had wielded,

Yvette came forward into the light from the smithy with the smith's son.

"Countess!" chided Thorolf. "I told you to hide in the woods!"

"One of my blood," she replied with dignity, "skulks not in hiding whilst her defenders risk their lives for her."

"A good thing she disobeyed you, Thorolf," growled the smith as he collected his hammers. "Without her aid, one or t'other of us would have gat a bolt in's brisket."

Thorolf was kneeling to examine the bodies. He rose, saying, "This one, too, seems safely dead. Let's pile the carrion out back and cover them. The constables will take them in charge after I report to them on the morrow. That was a mighty blow for one so delicate, Countess."

"The strength of desperation, I ween," said Yvette. Pointing to the corpse in the surcoat, she added: "I know that knave: a captain of Gondomar's guard. If you turn back his coat, you will see the red boar of Landai. His survivors will flee back to the Duke, who will set another party on my trail. Ere they return, you must discover me a wizard who can change my appearance, so I cannot be readily tracked. Couldst lead me to the one in Zurshnitt, whereof you told me, this very night?"

"Nay, my lady," said the soldier. "It's above an hour hence to town. All doors are already latched and barred. We must tarry here till dawn on a patch of floor with, perchance, a mattress and a coverlet from our friend."

"Better yet," said Vulfilac. "Your Ladyship shall have my bed!"

"A generous offer," she said, patting a yawn. "I am fordone. May I see this bed?"

"Up this ladder, madam."

Yvette, carrying her coronet, and Thorolf climbed

into the loft, the smith following with a candle. Yvette said: "A vasty bed, Goodman Vulfilac."

"My wife's and mine. Now I sleep with the lad; but he shall make do elsewhere, as shall I."

"So huge a bed with but one small occupant were wasteful and ridiculous. One of you shall take the other half."

Thorolf and Vulfilac exchanged glances. Thorolf said: "It would grieve me to oust a friend from's bed. I'll take the floor."

"Nay!" boomed the smith. "As host I have the final say, and I assign myself to the floor."

They argued until Yvette said: "A pox upon your courtesies! I've camped in the field with my soldiers, so bed sharing is nought new to me. My judgment is that you shall flip a coin."

The coin gave Thorolf the bed. Yvette stripped off her garments and pulled the coronet firmly down on her head.

Vulfilac, blushing above his beard, looked away. Thorolf exclaimed: "Countess! That's how I first met you. Do you sleep with that thing on?"

"Certes, as do many nobles and royals, to be sure their baubles be not stolen whilst they snore."

"Is it not uncomfortable?"

"One gets used to it, as you are accustomed to strutting about with a sword banging your shins. . . . Thorolf! You shall not get into my bed with those dirty clothes! Strip down like a man of sense!"

"You mean—ah—"

"Nay, silly, I make no lewd advances; my person is off-limits to commoners. Lend me that great knife of yours!"

"Not to stab me asleep, I hope?"

"Nay; but if I feel something poking me in the midsection, I shall know what to do. Good night!"

II

The Senescent Sorcerer

Tired though he was, Thorolf found sleep hard to come by. It seemed to him that he was just dropping off when he was aware of light and motion. He found Yvette already dressed, winding cloths around the coronet. He said:

"Sleep well, Countess?"

"Not so well as sometimes, with you tossing and turning all night."

The soldier reddened. "Your pardon. I fear the contiguity of one so fair. . . ."

"No need to apologize; at least it proves you no effeminate. Vulfilac yonder snores like a sawmill. Do not folk of his class rise early?"

Thorolf smiled. "Not when they've spent half the night rescuing penniless damsels from their pursuers!"

Breakfasted and mounted again, Thorolf turned his horse toward Zurshnitt. Clad in the smith's wife's feast-day finery, Yvette sat pillion behind him on the mare. On her head she wore her coronet so wrapped in cloth as to seem a turban. Out of sight of the smithy, Thorolf said:

"We must needs deposit that golden hoop safely and descend upon Doctor Bardi. But first I have my duties—"

"Not so, Sergeant! The care of me and my small treasure should come first."

"Sorry, my dear, but I cannot—"

"And what preëmpts my orders, sirrah?"

"First I must needs report to barracks and get leave for the day. Then I must visit the Constabulary about last night's fracas and the corpses we left at the smithy."

"Marry come up! The wishes of one of my rank—"

"Mean nought in Rhaetia, since you are but one more titled refugee, entitled to kind treatment but no mastership."

"But I insist—"

"It's a long walk to Zurshnitt," growled Thorolf. Yvette subsided. After a while she burst out:

"It is so unfair that I, a descendant of a hundred kings and princes, should have to beg and wheedle for what is mine by right! Means it nought that I am a direct, legitimate descendant of the hero-king, Ricolf the Third?"

Thorolf grinned. "But if you claim credit for the good deeds of King Ricolf, then you must accept blame for the crimes of the mad King Leodast, who murdered his parents and then burned all those people. Certes, if we hanged everyone with a murderer in's pedigree, not enough would survive to bury the bodies!"

"Master Thorolf, I wish no more of your irksome speech!"

"Aye-aye, your Highness!" With his most irritating chuckle, Thorolf fell silent.

Smelling of decades' accumulation of dust, Doctor Bardi's sanctum resembled a small-town museum into which heterogeneous objects had been crowded far beyond the room's capacity. A human skeleton grinned whitely from a corner. Shelves were jam-packed with books. Atop these volumes lay others on their sides; and on this makeshift shelving reposed skulls, limb bones, mineral specimens, the stuffed or dried remains of various creatures, and dusty bottles, jars, and jugs. More flotsam from the past hung from the ceiling; as he entered, Thorolf hit his head on a small stuffed crocodile.

After introductions, Yvette turned on her formidable charm. "Thorolf has told me much of you," she said to Bardi with a winning smile. "Do you live here all alone?"

"Aye, save for a woman who comes in betimes to clean and cook. Every moon or so she is seized by a passion to tidy up my house. After such a purification, I can never find the book or scroll I need. And now, my dears, if ye would not have me add the time spent in polite persiflage to my fee, let us to business."

"Dear me!" wheezed the ancient iatromage after learning his visitors' problems. " 'Tis a bit out of my line; I do not command deltas nor yet give rubbish the semblance of gold. But whereas Thorolf asks, I will do what I can. Ye say ye wish the look of a short, dark, dumpy female, eh? Dear me. Shall this be merely an illusion or glamor? Or would ye that I truly change your nature?"

"What are the virtues and faults of each proceeding?" Yvette asked.

"The illusion is easily cast and cheap; but it is banished as easily. A drop of wine or beer in the eyes were enough to reveal the true appearance of the ensorcelled one, as will a view of the subject in a mirror. The true change requires a more difficult and costly spell, and it will not soon reverse itself without an additional operation. Moreover, those who undergo it complain that it causes pain during the actual change."

"I choose the true change," said Yvette. "How long can I count upon its endurance?"

23

"For six months to a year, unless ye cause me or another to cast the reversing spell sooner. For, I must add, the usual fee."

"Charge the cost to Master Thorolf," said Yvette airily. "He knows I shall repay him when I recover my land." She smiled at Thorolf. "That's understood, is it not?"

Thorolf understood nothing of the kind; in fact he had been wondering how Bardi's services were to be paid for. He opened his mouth to protest, but so regal was Yvette's demeanor that nothing came out but a feeble, "Well—ah—"

"Good! That's settled," said the Countess. "When shall we begin, learned Doctor?"

"Forthwith; but the preparations will take—dear me—above an hour." Bardi stepped to a set of bookshelves, moved a dried human head encumbering the books, and pulled out an ancient folio. He blew dust off it, causing Thorolf to sneeze; put it back, and fumbled for another.

"Can we be done by dinner time?" asked Thorolf.

"Assuredly." The mage pulled out another volume.

"One other matter, Doctor," said Thorolf when he had blown his nose. "Show him the coronet, Countess."

Thorolf explained the need for a safe hiding place for the object. Bardi agreed to give it, too, a magical disguise and keep it in his custody until a more lasting arrangement could be made.

An hour and a half later, they watched as the old iatromage puttered about a pentacle drawn in charcoal on the floor. Five black candles had been set in the corners of the pentagram, casting a shimmery, greenish light around the otherwise darkened room.

"There!" said the magus, wiping his charcoal-stained hands on his black, symbol-spangled robe. "If ye'll take yon seats, my dears, we shall commence." He put away his spectacles, fumbled for another pair, and opened a volume.

24

The next hour was, for Thorolf, the mixture of tedium and apprehension that every lengthy magical operation aroused in him, much like the sensations of a soldier awaiting the command to advance. Bardi chanted in unknown tongues, made passes with a wand, and shouted names to summon unseen presences. The lighting dimmed; the space within the pentacle was filled with fog or smoke.

Thorolf thought he could discern substantial forms—colored russet, rose, yellow, and aquamarine—moving within. There were momentary hints of faces, limbs, and tentacles; but they shifted, dissolved, and reassembled in different configurations before he could perceive a substantial shape. He felt a prickling at the roots of his hair, as if an army of ants were crawling over him. A sidelong glance showed Yvette leaning back with her eyes closed, breathing heavily.

After what seemed hours, Bardi cried a dismissal. The fog in the pentacle faded. One candle guttered. The iatromage scuffed a couple of lines of the pentacle.

"That is it," he croaked. "My dears, ye may now go about your affairs. Remember that, about midnight, the lady will swiftly become short, dark, and dumpy. And now good night, for so powerful a spell doth tax one of my years."

Leading Salnia with one hand and supporting Yvette's arm with the other, Thorolf walked along the rounded cobbles, slippery with drizzle. Darkness had fallen; the watchfires at the main crossings gave a flickering, rubescent light. Two men of the Constabulary, with halberds on their shoulders, greeted Thorolf. One called:

"Hey, be this our virtuous sergeant on a tryst at last?"

"Nay," growled Thorolf. "Know, knaves, that this be the rightful Queen of Armoria, and we plot to oust the usurper."

Thorolf stopped before the Green Dragon Inn, where he was known. In the light of the lantern over the door,

Yvette looked puzzled. Then her face cleared. "Oh, *I* see! You did but jest about my rank. I thank you for the promotion." She giggled.

"Better late than never," said Thorolf. "I'll essay to get you a private room."

"Oh, fiddle-dee-dee! Where mean you to sleep?"

"Back at the barracks."

"Rubbish, my good Sergeant! Think you, when I'm fleeing Gondomar the Tedious and have by good hap found a lusty bodyguard, that I'd let him go off leaving me defenseless? You shall spend the night with me, and that is that. Sleep on the floor if you will, but you shall stay within sight and call. The Queen of Armoria commands it!"

Thus they found themselves in what, Thorolf thought, must be the room that Vasco the innkeeper reserved for nobility. The bed was big enough for three, and there was plenty of room besides. There was a dressing table and a mirror, a dressing chair, and a settee, as well as a writing desk with another chair. Such splendor, Thorolf thought, had resulted from Yvette's queenly demand:

"Your very best, Master Taverner!"

Thorolf left the room to Yvette while he washed off the grime of travel in the common bathtub. Escorting her to dinner, he found himself unconsciously assuming the toplofty air of a nobleman to match her born-to-command manner. That and her courtly accent had reduced even the experienced Vasco to subservience despite Yvette's proletarian costume. When they were seated, Vasco produced a dusty bottle, saying:

"Firanzian, third year of Consul Rudolf. Will it suit your Ladyship?"

"Belike it will," she said. "Let's have a trial."

When the wine was poured, Yvette took a sizable mouthful. "Aha!" she said. "This is an improvement over Goodman Vulfilac's small beer—not that I scorn the honest fellow's hospitality."

Over dinner, Yvette entertained Thorolf with tales of

26

courtly scandals in the New Neapolitan Empire. She rattled out as much in a minute as most folk did in five. Thorolf found her talk fascinating, though he sometimes wished he could get a word in edgewise.

He also noted, with rising alarm, her execution on the bottle of costly wine. By the end of the repast it was all gone, and Thorolf was sure that she had drunk more of it than he.

He noted another thing. There were two other tables of diners in the common room. These had somehow gotten wind of the fact that Thorolf was with a noble lady. They turned in their seats to stare until Thorolf scowled them into averting their gaze.

The other diners had departed; Thorolf was wiping his mouth and preparing to rise when Yvette said: "Oh, linger an instant, Thorolf! Master Taverner, hast some water-of-life in stock?"

"Aye, your Ladyship," said Vasco.

"Then fetch a noggin apiece, pray."

"Countess," said Thorolf, "think you not that you've had enough?"

"My good Sergeant, I have been on the run for days, and this is my first chance to take my ease in a duck's age! Thank you, Mashter—Master Taverner."

She tossed down the colorless schnapps with a single gulp, while Thorolf drank his by sips. Then she fixed him with a purposeful stare. "Tell me, dear rescuer, what meant those yokels of the nightwatch, chaffing you about their virtuous sergeant? I mean, when you clept me Queen of Armoria." She giggled.

"Merely," said Thorolf uncomfortably, "that they have not seen me strolling with the strumpets of the town, as they have many of mine unwed soldier lads."

Yvette's glance became sharp. "Are you one of those unlucky ones whose passions veer toward their own sex?"

"Kernun forbid! I am as avid for womankind as any."

"Well, then, an you roll not the local trollops, hast a

27

regular light o' love whom you visit for a bout betwixt sheets?''

"Nay, none." Thorolf stared at his noggin, increasingly embarrassed by the direction of the questions.

"Then whom have you fuf-futtered?"

Thorolf gulped, his wits slowed by drink. The question appalled him; it was certainly not what he had been brought up to consider ladylike. On the other hand, with this masterful woman, he feared he could never get away with the pretense of ever having been a great lover. He blurted:

"Well—in sooth—I haven't."

"*What?* How old are you?"

"Twenty-nine."

"Three more years than I, a man of normal urgings—or so you say—and a *virgin*? 'Tis a thing incredible. In Carinthia they'd put you in a curio cabinet." She beckoned Vasco and ordered another round of *aqua vitae*.

"Really, Countess," said Thorolf, "you will rue your overindulgence—"

"No one tells the daughter of a hundred kings and nobles what to do! But back to your case. What's the caush of your unwonted abstinence?"

Thorolf gulped again. "Well, if you must know, I promised my mother on her deathbed not to fornicate before marriage. I once got as far as betrothal to the daughter of our senior sergeant; but she forsook me for one who, I ween, was less scrupulous."

She drank more schnapps and giggled. "Sh—serves you right! What a pity that yours be a lower-class organ! I could give you lessons—break you in—were not plebian organs forbidden my c—c—" She fell into a spell of hiccups.

Thorolf said, "Mean you—ah—that you've had much experience of such things?"

She got her hiccups under control. "What thinkst? We of the true nobility make no holy idol of chast—" The hiccups broke in again.

Fearing that she would pass out or get publicly sick, Thorolf spoke sharply, in the tone he used on stumbling recruits: "Come, Yvette! Let me take you to bed!"

He half-forcibly dragged her out of her seat and guided her, staggering, to the stair. Here she became so unsteady that he picked her up and carried her to the room. When he would have laid her on the bed, she said:

"Put me down, Thorolf! I am hale; but tell nobody that I cannot hold my liquor. 'Twas jush the fatigue of recent days."

When her feet came to the floor, she pulled Thorolf, clutching his arm and staggering, to the settee. There she pushed him down, sat on his lap, and kissed him vigorously. "There! Izh—isn't that better?"

"Well—ah—"

She kissed him some more. "Now you shall learn what you should have found out years agone."

"Methought you said—"

"Ne'mind what I shaid. I'm a noblewoman and can bed anyone I like. Besides, I'm in your debt, and debts mush be paid. Since I cannot fill your hat with g-gold . . ." Rising unsteadily, she did off the bodice, blouse, skirt, petticoat, and accessories. Leaving the garments borrowed from Vulfilac in a heap on the floor, in full pink-and-white glory she staggered back to Thorolf and fumbled with his laces, mumbling:

"Flinch not; I'll not hurt you. You actually blush!" She peeled off Thorolf's shirt. "Now your breeks. . . . Aha, I see you have indeed the means. . . ."

"I only hope I can meet your expectations," said Thorolf.

"Fear not; if our first firsh try come to nought. . . ." As she pulled off the last of Thorolf's linen small-clothes, she broke off, dropped the underwear, and fell into a sitting position on the settee. "Thorolf, I feel very strange of a sudden!"

"After all that liquor—" he began sententiously.

"But then, too, it must be close to the time for Bardi's spell to take effect."

"Oh, I had forgotten! Wilt still love me, even though I become dark and dumpy? I shall still be the same. . . . Ouch! I am in pain. . . . glub—"

As Thorolf gazed with mounting horror, the slight, golden-haired woman changed before his eyes. Her voice sounded like the bubbling of gas through swamp water and then ceased. She seemed to flow together. Her limbs became limp, as if their bones had dissolved. Her face lost form and sank into her body.

Thorolf shrank back, for the thing on the settee was no longer remotely human. Its parts shifted into a completely alien configuration. The limbs and eyes migrated to one end, leaving the torso a mere fleshy bag.

The four limbs split lengthwise to form eight, which became sucker-lined tentacles. They surrounded the mouth, which acquired a short, horny beak. The skin changed to a shiny, mottled, dark-brown integument, over which rippled flashes of red, yellow, white, and black. The Countess had become an octopus.

Thorolf sat paralyzed. When he gathered his bare legs beneath him to spring up, the octopus whipped tentacles around his neck and hoisted its bag of a body into his lap. It pressed its beak against his bare chest, but it did not bite him; it merely touched his skin lightly here and there. Thorolf realized that it was trying to kiss him.

To be seduced by a drunken octopus was, he thought, not a fate that befalls many. If he survived this night, he would have a tale he could dine out on for years; but just now he would gladly forgo the experience.

"Yvette!" he cried. The octopus continued to snuggle, as if she expected him to continue the project on which they had embarked. But not only did Thorolf have no idea of how to do this, his lust had also collapsed like a tent blown down in a gale.

He shouted, still without effect. Then he realized that, as a sea creature, the octopus lacked the organs for hearing and speech. How, he frantically wondered, could he communicate?

At last the octopus slithered off his lap. With serpentine tentacular writhings, it heaved itself across the room to the dressing table, while changes of color, white to tan to brown to black, rippled over its shiny skin. Finding locomotion out of water hard, it clambered laboriously up on the dressing chair and stared at its reflection in the mirror. The image was that of an octopus, proving that this change was no mere glamor or illusion.

Then the octopus slid off the chair with a plop and humped and wriggled to the washstand. There it picked up the pitcher and, its tentacles quivering with strain, tipped the vessel over itself, so that water splashed over its body and trickled to the floor. It dropped the empty pitcher, swiveled about to face Thorolf, and waved its tentacles, pointing a couple of them at the pitcher. It seemed to be trying to say something; but with neither lungs nor an agreed-upon sign language, it failed.

Next, it slithered to the writing desk and, groping about on the desktop, located the inkwell. It dipped the tip of a tentacle into the ink and wrote on the wall in large, crude letters: WATER.

Of course, Thorolf thought, such a marine creature could not long survive in air. But how to succor it? He could not stand pouring pitcher after pitcher over it. The water would leak through the floor and bring Vasco on the run. And whence would come such a supply of water?

The octopus seemed to divine his thought. Again it dipped the tentacle and wrote: TUB.

Light broke upon Thorolf. He nodded, hastily pulled on his shirt and trews, and went below to find Vasco. To the innkeeper he said:

"My lady demands a bath. Will your people haul up a tub and several bucketfuls of water?"

"Sergeant!" said Vasco. "Why can she not bathe in the perfectly good tub at the end of the hall, as ye did aforetime?"

"She's high-born and fussy," said Thorolf. "She insists on utter privacy."

" 'Twill cost extra," the taverner warned. "And 'twill take an hour to heat the water."

"The water need not be heated."

"A rugged wench," Vasco muttered.

Back in the room, Thorolf signaled that he had succeeded. He opened the door of the wardrobe and motioned Yvette to enter. She was barely concealed therein when a knock announced the arrival of the squirrel-toothed potboy and the maid, lugging a large wooden tub. They set it down and eyed Thorolf curiously before departing for the water. They soon returned, each bearing two buckets. When these had been emptied into the tub, the potboy asked: "Be that enough, sir?"

Thorolf looked into the tub. "Nay; we need four buckets more."

When four additional buckets had been emptied, Thorolf said, "Methinks that will do."

The maid went out, but the potboy hung around saying: "Will there be aught else, sir?" His youthful glance roamed the room. He must be puzzled, Thorolf thought, not to see Yvette. Either he is angling for a tip or hoping to glimpse a noble lady at her bath. "Well, sir, an ye think of aught else—"

The door of the wardrobe flew open, and Yvette slithered across the floor. The sound of life-giving water had plainly put upon her self-restraint more stress than it could withstand.

As the octopus whipped a tentacle over the edge of the tub, the potboy stared with bulging eyes. When Yvette slid bonelessly into the tub with a small splash, the potboy fled with piercing shrieks.

Thorolf closed the door and looked into the tub. Yvette lay flattened down on the bottom like a cluster of hibernating serpents, with the water covering all but her eyes.

The eyes that gazed up at Thorolf had slit pupils like those of a cat, but the slits were horizontal instead of vertical.

A tentacle snaked out of the tub. For an instant, Thorolf wondered if he would be seized and pulled in, though for what purpose he could only guess. He braced himself to resist, but the tentacle merely stroked and patted his chest, as if to show affection.

Footsteps sounded, and Thorolf heard Vasco's knock. He narrowly opened the door and slipped out, firmly holding the knob to cut off the view of the room.

"Yea, Master Vasco?" he said with an air of innocent surprise.

"Sergeant," said Vasco, "my potboy just now came clattering down the stair, crying that a devil in the form of a monstrous spider had issued from the wardrobe and sprung at him. He raced off into the night."

"Oh, that," said Thorolf, thinking fast. "My lady had disrobed and secluded herself in the wardrobe. When the maid departed, she issued forth, supposing your boy had likewise gone. When she saw the stripling, she snatched my cloak and wrapped it about her."

Vasco rubbed his chin. "Very well, Sergeant, if ye say so. I do hope there be no wizardry connected with this. If the word got out, 'twere bad for my trade."

"Worry not," said Thorolf. "Meanwhile, pray give orders that none shall enter the room until we signify."

"I understand, Sergeant. Strength to your yard!" With a knowing leer, Vasco departed.

Thorolf returned to the room and sank down upon the settee, thinking. At last he rose and bent over the tub. Speaking with exaggerated lip movements, he said: "I go to visit Doctor Bardi again." When she lay quietly, he pointed to himself and then to the door. He pulled a coverlet off the bed, spread it over the tub, and left.

III
The Sinister Sect

"Dear me!" said Doctor Bardi, in nightgown and nightcap. "This is most unfortunate. What is this creature ye say the Countess hath become?"

"A polyp. I saw them in the fish markets when I studied at Genuvia. The Tyrrhenians eat them under the name of *polpo*."

"Meseems not like gourmet fare. Hast ever partaken thereof?"

"Aye, once. It tastes not unlike other seafood, save that the one I ate must have been a tough old monster marine. It was like chewing rawhide bootlaces. I learned much at Genuvia, but not what to do when my sweetling becomes a creature of the deep. What wilt do about it?"

Bardi nodded thoughtfully. "Tell me, did the Countess partake of any intoxicating beverage betwixt the time I cast the spell and that when it took effect?"

"Sink me in Lake Zurshnitt, but did she drink! She outdrank me, with but half my bulk. By the time we returned to the room, she was as drunk as a Locanian lord. Forsooth, she even forgot her aristocratic interdictions against carnal commerce with commoners and set about seducing me! She'd have succeeded handily, too, had not this change come upon her. But what—"

Bardi struck his palm against his forehead. "Ah, the penalties of age! Thorolf, I meant to warn you twain that she must not touch any alcoholic liquor, even small beer, until after the change hath taken place."

"Well, why didst not?"

"I forgot! Ah, woe is me! Since this contretemps is in part my fault, I'll charge but half my regular fee—"

Thorolf roared: "You'll charge for turning my beautiful countess into an eight-legged sea monster? Go futter yourself! Not a penny shall you have; and you shall repair your error or face a suit for magical malpractice!"

Bardi recoiled. "Dear me! From what ye say, the lady hath suffered no lasting scathe. An I can restore her proper form, I shan't have harmed her. Belike I had better view her myself. Wait whilst I dress."

He vanished into the bedroom and soon reappeared in his symbol-spangled gown, saying: "Now, where did I put my cap?"

Bardi rummaged through his clutter and eventually located his headgear resting on the dried human head. It was an academic skullcap of stiff black material, atop which was fixed a square of the same material embellished with a dangling purple tassel.

At the inn, Thorolf whisked the coverlet off the tub. "There she is. Believe it or not, that is the veritable Yvette of Grintz. You made her short, dark, and dumpy with a vengeance, and at a most inconvenient time."

The wizard had been breathing hard from keeping up with Thorolf's soldierly stride. He gave a dry chuckle.

"Oh, ye were just about to . . . Ah, to be ninety again!
At least it's better than if she had turned werewolf."

Bardi fell silent while changing his eyeglasses, more
closely to scrutinize Yvette, who waved a tentacle in
greeting. At last he sighed.

"My good Sergeant, I fear ye've set me a task beyond
my poor powers. The counterspell calls for some of the
rare ingredients of the original, and I lack more of these.
It might take a year or more to replace them."

"Mean you she must remain a polyp till then?"

"Nay. There are others of the fraternity of greater
puissance than I. Surely one of those can reverse the
spell."

"Name one."

"The ablest for this, in my judgment, were the Great
Psychomage, Doctor Orlandus."

"The Sophonomist? That were like begging aid from
a tiger when fleeing a lion. I suspect Orlandus be more
wind and boastery than true ability. It's rumored that
his doctorate, even, be not genuine but self-conferred.
I'd liefer consult Doctor Tetricus at the college; he is
one of the few who backed me in the Dorelian trouble."

"But Tetricus is on sabbatical leave, is he not?"

"Oh," said Thorolf. "I had forgotten."

"So I am not the only one, ye see." The iatromage
shrugged. "From all I can gather, Orlandus is not a
man to be trusted overmuch; but of his genuine wiz-
ardly powers there is no doubt. All I know for sure is
that Orlandus' followers report amazing cures. One
ninny, who never finished four grades of schooling, so
augmented his powers that from the sound of a footfall
he could tell the sex, age, weight, and general aspect
of the walker. Orlandus claims that he who takes his
full course can acquire such godlike powers; he calls
such a one a 'diaphane.' "

"I've heard of them. Hast ever met such a demigod?"

"Nay; but others tell me thereof, for whatever the tales may be worth." Bardi spread his hands. "I have told you all I can, Sergeant. This metamorphosis is particularly difficult to reverse, requiring a magician of the highest powers. Otherwise she might not recover her natural form for months or even years. I can but urge you to hie yourself and the Countess to Castle Hill and bespeak Orlandus' aid—with due caution, certes."

"How shall I get the Countess from this inn without causing a riot?"

The aged mage furrowed his brow. "Could those who fetched the tub hither take it down the stair—unaware of its contents?"

Thorolf grasped a corner of the tub and, with a grunt, heaved it upward. The corner rose a hand's breadth, while the water sloshed about. Yvette moved uneasily in the tub, while color changes flickered over her mottled hide.

"With the water and Yvette," said Thorolf, "it must weigh two hundred or more. Vasco's domestics could never manage it; nor could I alone. It's an awkward shape to carry. Hast no levitation spell to lighten our labors?"

"Alas!" sighed Bardi. "In my youth I could levitate a hundredweight as featly as ye raise a spoonful of pottage; but with age my psychokinetic powers have dwindled. How if we hired brawny workers and fastened poles to the tub for carrying? Or better yet, run it out the window on a boom or crane and lower it by rope?"

Thorolf shook his head. "Vasco would never let us make so free with his tub."

"Ye could buy him a better."

"But in the course of this cheaping and chaffering, Yvette's transformation would surely come to light and cause a turmoil. And once we got the tub to the ground, what then? Carry her in my arms, or ask her to wriggle along the cobblestones after me like a faithful dog? We should have a mob of Zurshnitters running and shrieking like the fiends of the Dualist Hell. Whilst I know not how long these sea creatures survive out of water, I dare not expose her to the atmosphere longer than can be helped.''

"Well, then," creaked Bardi, "wherefore not buy another tub, hire a carter, place the tub in his cart, and fill it with water? Then ye can lower the Countess by a bedsheet from the window.''

"Canst imagine what the good folk of Zurshnitt would think, if they saw a monstrous polyp climbing down the sheet by its tentacles? Besides which, the terrified carter would flee ere she reached the ground.''

Bardi sighed. "It would simplify matters an ye boiled her up and ate her, as ye say they do in Tyrrhenia.''

"An ill-timed jest," growled Thorolf. "I may not be a perfect gentle knight of romance, but I have some sense of responsibility. I have it! We'll buy the tub, rent the cartage, and I shall carry Yvette out wrapped in a wet bedsheet. I'll tell Vasco that the Countess be departed, and this bundle be the dirty linens from our travels, which I am taking to the washerwoman.''

" 'Twould require a journey to Pantorozia and back, not a day's fishing, to accumulate so much wash," said the mage doubtfully.

"Cannot be helped. Now we shall catch a wink of slumber." Thorolf pulled off his boots. "Luckily the bed is big enough for the twain. You're not the bedmate I should have chosen; but if you thrash about not, we shall manage.''

With the first dawnlight, Thorolf yawned, stretched, and came fully awake. He found Bardi already up, sitting on the dressing chair and trimming his fingernails. Thorolf pulled on his boots, saying:

"I'm off, Doctor, and may be gone some small time. You shall remain to guard the door and keep Yvette company whilst I seek the needfuls. For reasons I need not recapitulate, I expect you to pay for these purchases.''

"Such a mercenary springald!" grumped Bardi. "A warrior true is a reckless spendthrift.''

"I profess not to be a warrior true; I save to pay for the professors' fees when I study for my doctorate. And tell that to my father, who ever chides me on my lack of proper Rhaetian rapacity! So pay me now!'' With a menacing scowl, Thorolf presented his palm.

"Dear me!" Grumbling, Bardi fumbled in his purse. "How much?"

"Ten marks should cover."

"But what shall I do for food?" queried the ancient. "Your Countess, likewise, will require aliment.''

"You could climb into the tub and let her breakfast on you, if your tissues prove not too tough and stringy.''

"Now who makes jokes in ill-taste? I'm sure she would find a plump fish more to her liking.''

"I'll fetch you a bun and the Countess a fish," said Thorolf. "I'll tell Vasco that my lady be ill of a contagious disease, wherefor you are treating her; and his folk must on no account enter herein. That is no great falsehood, either.''

"One thing more," said Bardi. "The polyp, I infer, is a creature of the sea. When ye fill this other tub, add a spoonful of salt, for your lady's health.''

Noon was nigh when Thorolf returned. He handed Bardi his bun, unwrapped a carp, and dropped it into the tub. A tentacle whipped the fish out of sight beneath the umbrella of arms.

When mage and monster had finished their repasts, Thorolf gathered up the sheet and dipped it into the water. With Bardi's help, he spread it out on the floor and motioned Yvette to climb out on it.

She seemed reluctant to leave the water but at last appeared to grasp the idea. Over the edge she came, first writhing tentacles, then slit-pupiled eyes, and at last the bulky, boneless bag of a body. She coiled herself into a mottled brown lump on the sheet, watching Thorolf with unwinking stare as he made a small bundle of Yvette's garments, borrowed from Vulfilac the smith.

Thorolf gathered the corners of the sheet and tied them together into a bag. He picked up the improvised sack.

"Is she heavy?" asked Bardi.

"No more than when she was human, which is to say a little above a hundred. Come along!"

They went down with Thorolf cradling the bundle. Vasco appeared, saying: "How doth your lady, Sergeant? Ye told me she ailed."

"Much better now, thanks to Doctor Bardi. She's already gone forth. The good Doctor will pay the scot, and your sheet shall be returned on the morrow."

Thorolf strode out, leaving a quietly fuming Bardi fumbling in his purse. The cart stood beneath the tub, to the sides of which were affixed handles for carrying.

Bardi appeared, saying: "Is that all, Sergeant? I'm fain to return to my sanctum."

"Nay, sir!" said Thorolf sternly. "You shall remain with me until we have delivered her."

He climbed up on the wheel of the cart and dumped his bundle into the tub, saying to the carter in the local dialect: "This is a rare fish, meant as a gift to the King of Carinthia if we can keep it alive. Goodman Wentz, wilt take a look at your mule's off rear foot? Methought it limped a trifle on our way hither."

Cursing under his breath, the carter climbed down from his perch and examined the hoof. While he did so, Thorolf untied the corners of the sheet and pulled it out from under Yvette. He spread the sheet over the tub.

"Nought amiss here," the carter grumbled, resuming his place.

"Good; let's go!"

* * *

Long before, when Rhaetia had been under the kings of Carinthia, the kings' servants had erected a frowning castelet on a hill in the midst of Zurshnitt, to house the garrison and overawe the citizens. Since independence, Zurshnitt had grown far beyond its former boundaries. Left derelict, Zurshnitt Castle had been bought and refurbished by the Order of Sophonomy.

Thorolf and Bardi walked through the Street of Clockmakers to the base of Castle Hill, followed by the cart. When the slope steepened, the mule balked until Thorolf put his massive shoulder to the tail of the cart and pushed. The street became a winding path to the castle gate.

The curtain wall with its corner turrets was made of a gray gneiss, in which flakelets of mica sparkled in the sunshine. Reaching the gate of Zurshnitt Castle slightly out of breath, Thorolf saw a pair of chain-mailed guards in azure livery standing stiffly at attention. As the cart approached, these two crossed halberds with a clang before it. One said brusquely:

"State your business, sir!"

Thorolf noticed that the swords worn by these two were not belayed to their scabbards by peace wires, as required of the civilians of Zurshnitt. He said: "We have the victim of a spell gone awry, and we are told that Doctor Orlandus can cure such maladies."

"Who is this victim?" snapped the guard. "Is it ye?"

"Nay; she's in the tub. It is vital to keep her covered."

The guard glowered. "Think ye we'd let such a mysterious load into our headquarters uninspected? Ye maun be daft! Uncover it, Crasmund!"

"Ho!" cried Thorolf. "Don't—"

The other guard had already seized a corner of the sheet. Now he whipped it off and stared into the tub. He reeled back with a shriek: "A demon! A demon!"

41

"What?" cried the other guard, pushing forward for a look. "Nay, 'tis a monster!"

The carter gave a squeal like that of a rusty hinge, leaped down from his seat, and ran.

"A demon, I say!" yelled the first guard.

"Nay, a monster!" shouted the second.

"A demon!"

"A monster!"

"A demon, as any nullwit can see!"

"Fools!" roared Thorolf. "It's my patient, for Doctor Orlandus to treat!"

"Demon or monster, I'll send it back to its native hell!" screamed the first guard, raising his halberd to thrust at Yvette with the spearhead on the end.

"Stop!" yelled Thorolf. He sprang toward the first guard and seized the shaft of the halberd below the ax head. "You idiots, that's the Countess of Grintz, ensorceled!"

"Ha!" snorted the first guard, wrestling with Thorolf for possession of the halberd. "I once met a countess, when I soldiered for the Count of Treveria, and she looked not at all like this! Guard! Turn out!"

With a mighty wrench, Thorolf tore the weapon from the guard. Losing his grip on the shaft, the guard, backed against the side of the cart, reached for his sword. He had it half out of the scabbard when a mottled, brown-and-white tentacle snaked out of the tub, caught him round the neck, and dragged him shrieking over the edge.

Sensing motion behind him, Thorolf whirled to meet the other guard. The man swung his halberd in a decapitating blow. Thorolf knew that, while the swing of this top-heavy weapon was slow enough to be usually evaded or parried, when such a blow got home it commonly killed. He also knew that he fought at a disadvantage. While the guards seemed eager to kill him, he did not wish to slay either and thus foreclose all chance of help from Orlandus.

He caught the swing of the other halberd on the head of the one in his hands. The ax heads met with a hideous clang. Instead of retaliating in kind, Thorolf reversed his shaft and rammed the butt into the guard's solar plexus. The coat of mesh mail and the padded acton beneath did little to break the force of the thrust; the man went sprawling on the cobbles, doubled up and clutching his midriff.

Thorolf turned to glimpse the carter in flight down the path up which they had come, and Doctor Bardi crawling under the cart. The legs of the guard whose halberd Thorolf had taken dangled kicking over the edge of the tub, while from the tub came the bubbling sounds of a man trying to shout with his face under water.

"What in the seven hells betides?" shouted another armored man, an officer from his scarlet insignia, issuing from the portal at the head of a squad of blue-clad guards.

"I came to present a patient for Doctor Orlandus to treat—" began Thorolf.

The felled guard, who had stopped coughing, climbed to his feet and cried: "He—he seeks to smuggle a monster into the castle!"

"Give up your weapons, and we'll look into this matter," the officer growled.

"No, sir, I will not! I am a soldier of the Rhaetian Army, and those idiots attacked me without provocation."

"What doth my man in yon tub?" asked the officer.

"My patient, who is in the tub, came to mine aid," Thorolf said, leaning the halberd against the cart and pulling the barely conscious guard out by the legs. Thorolf turned him over, hoisted him by the middle, and shook the water out of him. The man went into an agony of coughing.

The officer stepped to the tub. "*That's* your patient?"

"Aye; she's a noble lady under enchantment."

43

"Ha!" said the officer. "When I believe that, I shall believe the legend that Arnalt of Thessen rode his horse across Lake Zurshnitt atop the waves."

"Ah, Sergeant Thorolf of the Fourth Foot, I believe!" said a new voice from the gateway. The cluster of guards opened out as the newcomer approached. As he passed among them, they placed hands over their hearts and bowed low.

The object of their reverence was a tall, lean man with a long, mobile face, wherein slanting eyebrows and greenish-blue eyes effected a slightly eerie look. He wore a scarlet robe of shimmering stuff. Upon his midnight mane of long black hair reposed a golden academic cap, whose dangling tassel glinted with little gems.

"Who is that beneath the cart?" demanded the newcomer. "Ah, I do perceive my respected colleague, Doctor Bardi. Come out, my dear fellow! None shall harm a hair of your venerable head."

Brushing dirt from his robe, Bardi arduously rose. "I am sorry, Doctor Orlandus," he coughed, stooping to pick up his mortarboard. "Dear me! I fear that I be too old for the robustious games your minions play. Had ye not appeared so timely, they would have harmed far more than the hairs of our heads."

He finished brushing his cap and ceremoniously raised it to the Psychomage, who in turn tipped his cap to Bardi before he strode to the tub.

"Who was this when she had her normal form?" he asked in a mellifluous voice.

"Countess Yvette of Grintz," said Thorolf. "Bardi tried to alter her appearance, the better to elude her foes; but something went awry."

"Ah, yea; the widow of Count Volk. A woman of exceptional qualities; she could easily become a diaphane, thus enhancing her already notable powers. *Our* spells never miscarry thus." He turned to his guardsmen. "Captain, tell four men to bear this tub within.

44

Choose another to fetch fodder for the mule, and guard the cart until the carter return for his property. Now follow me, my dear friends.''

As they walked leisurely under the raised portcullis, Orlandus continued: "Your Countess escaped from Duke Gondomar with nought but a horse, her garments, and her coronet, did she not? And presently lost both horse and clothes to her pursuers. Where is the coronet now?''

''In safekeeping,'' growled Thorolf suspiciously, glancing about.

On the inner side of the curtain wall, many stairways led to the parapet. Between the stairways, casements had been built into the massive lower wall, forming living quarters. In the middle of the enclosure, separated from the curtain wall by a space of twenty or thirty feet all the way round, rose the keep, a massive, turreted building of rust-red sandstone. It overtopped the curtain wall by a whole storey. On the second and third levels, the present owners had replaced the arrow slits by diamond-paned glass windows.

As they crossed the courtyard, persons of various ages bustled out one door and in another. All wore robes, calf-length for the men and ankle-length for the women. Some were bright yellow and the rest gray, save for one or two in scarlet like that of the leader. Beyond, Thorolf glimpsed a couple of women in nondescript attire washing clothes in a tub and three small children playing. The guards' families, he thought.

In the midst of the yard, three men and two women in gray robes were on their knees, washing the cobblestones with scrubbing brushes and water buckets. As Thorolf passed these scrubbers, one of the women, young and pretty, looked up. At Orlandus' frown she hastily looked down again and resumed her labor.

They entered one of the massive doors of the keep and passed down a hall. Another young woman in gray

45

stood meekly aside as they entered and then resumed polishing the inside doorknob. Orlandus said:

"Ah, yea; my prudent sergeant would deposit Yvette's bauble safely, would he not? 'Twould fetch a pretty sum—belike twelve thousand marks."

He conducted them up a long stair, down the right-hand one of a pair of long halls, and into a spacious room, containing chairs, a divan, and a large desk. Seating himself behind the desk, Orlandus motioned Thorolf and Bardi to chairs. At another gesture, the soldiers set down the tub and departed.

Thorolf glanced around. In contrast to Bardi's dusty clutter, the chamber was as clean, neat, bare, and orderly as if it had never been occupied at all. The door through which they had come was one of a pair on one of the long sides of the room, which was cheerfully lit by diamond-paned casement windows at the ends. On the long side facing the doors was a low fireplace, but no fire had been laid and there were neither ashes nor cinders on the hearth.

Above the fireplace hung a huge framed painting, extending to the ceiling and dark with the dirt of decades. Through the grime it faintly showed the God and Goddess, Voth and Frea, of the Dualistic Church of Carinthia and the Empire. A small tear above Voth's head had not been repaired.

The Divine Pair had originally been painted seated on the natural thrones formed by a pair of thick-stemmed, twisted trees. The divinities extended benedictory hands above a multitude of tiny figures, representing mortal mankind, which swarmed about their feet. The Pair had originally been nude, Voth with a great black beard rippling down his chest and a wreath of laurel leaves on his hair; Frea as a beautiful blond woman of matronly figure. Someone had later painted bronze-green oak leaves over the Divine Couple's sexual characters.

Following Thorolf's glance, Orlandus said: "This

was the audience chamber of the Carinthian governors when they ruled in Rhaetia. When the Carinthians departed, they evidently found the moving of yon painting more trouble than they deemed it worth. According to a Tyrrhenian expert I had in, it is second-rate art. Still, it might be worth cleaning some day when we have the time.''

Thorolf said: "Here are the garments she wore ere her transformation." He laid the bundle on Orlandus' desk before sitting down. "I see you are not using the fireplace, Doctor, albeit winter will be upon us erelong."

Orlandus smiled. "The fireplace is more ornamental than useful. The castle hath an amenity invented in the days of the old Neapolitan Empire but neglected since. It is clept central heating. A furnace in the basement sends warm air through ducts to the far reaches of the building."

Another good-looking woman of about Yvette's age, also swathed in gray, entered and began mopping the floor, although Thorolf could not discern a speck of dust. He said:

"You keep a neat hold, Doctor."

"Surely. I am a modern, scientific magus. All operations are conducted in accordance with the latest principles of natural philosophy. One cannot be efficient without order."

Thorolf exchanged glances with Bardi, whose sanctum was at a polar extreme from their present surroundings. The soldier jerked his head towards the woman mopping. "Do your folk clean even when there is no dirt?"

Orlandus chuckled. "She serves a light sentence of expiation for a breach of discipline by a member of our order, of the lowest or probationary grade. Only when the aspirant hath risen to the rank of diaphane is he or she immune to such discipline. Since the recent warm spell hath made it needless to stoke the central furnace,

I have instead passed sentences of cleaning and polishing. A diaphane, however, knows the right thing to do on all occasions and does it.

"Let us return to the concomitants of my treatment of your Countess, since you expressed the desire that I do so. The price of the coronet would not nearly cover the cost of the Spell of Mimingus needed to restore Yvette to her winsome former self. You, Sergeant, have seven hundred-odd marks on deposit with Banker Virus, saved up for your tuition. And you, Doctor Bardi, have at least fifteen thousand in the hoard you secrete in your house."

"How knew you?" blurted Thorolf.

"Ah, what good were my arcane powers if I kept not abreast of my clients' affairs? Adding the sums from the coronet and your respective assets, that gives a total of about thirty thousand marks. Not nearly enough, I fear."

Thorolf bristled. "Meanst that you'd leave her in her polypose form if we cannot raise money beyond all we own?"

"My dear fellow! Take not so rigid a view. With a little adjustment, I am sure we can come to an amicable arrangement. I know somewhat of Yvette of Grintz, whose presence would much enhance my following. There is no rush about paying me all at once. I shall expect payment in installments of, let us say, one-tenth at a time, to allow you gentlemen time to arrange for loans.

"Meanwhile I shall keep Yvette here. Come back in a fortnight, with the first installment, and you shall find her restored. But she will not return to you until you have met the full cost of this difficult operation."

Thorolf thought privately that anyone who tried to hold Yvette against her will would find his work cut out for him. He said: "How would you stop her from leaving the castle?"

"Not by bars and shackles, I do assure you. She will

understand that she owes it to me to remain here until the costs of the operation be met. The total reckoning will be—ah—thirty-five thousand marks.''

"Ye'd beggar us!" grumbled Bardi.

"I am truly sorry, but this cannot be helped. Without resources I cannot carry on my great work for the benefit of mankind. Let it be agreed that one or the other shall return a fortnight hence with the first payment, thirty-five hundred marks, in good Rhaetian gold or silver." Orlandus rose. "Now let us part so that I can begin the arduous and costly preparations."

Taking each visitor by the elbow, Orlandus steered them to the gate, talking smoothly the while: "After this affair be wound up, my good Sergeant, I should welcome you as a subject for my mind-enhancing treatment. I do perceive you to be a man of great potential, combining the body of a mighty warrior with the mind of a scholar. This is a rare blend; we might even make a diaphane of you, could you stay the course."

"Gramercy for your compliments," said Thorolf. "But do your treatments require more money?"

"Certes! We cannot conduct this world-saving institution and maintain our headquarters and laboratories on air. But I am sure that arrangements can be effected, once you are enrolled amongst the followers of Sophonomy. We can rid you of all the fears and guilts accumulated in previous lives."

"For now," said Thorolf, "my obligation is to the Commonwealth and its Constitution. I'll do nought that conflicts with those."

"But of course, my dear fellow! Many of my people also give loyal service to the Commonwealth in various capacities." He spoke to a gate guard: "Where is the cart these gentlemen brought that tub in?"

"The carter returned and drave it off, Master," said the guard, placing a hand over his heart and bowing.

"Good! We are scrupulous in such affairs. We shall

discuss these matters further, Sergeant. And now, my friends, farewell. Remember, a fortnight hence!''

Leading his horse, Thorolf arrived at the barracks just as the morning's drill was being dismissed and the men were returning their pikes to the huge rack at the side of the drill ground. Captain Bothvar came up with a scowl like a thunderstorm, saying:

"Where in the seven hells have ye been, Thorolf? Your leave went only till muster time this morn. 'Tis not like you to vanish without leave.''

"A matter of honor, sir. A noble lady who besought my aid met with an accident, and there was none but I to obtain her the proper medical care.''

"Hmm. If ye say so, I daresay 'tis so. I put Sergeant Regin in your stead; ye can trade leaves with him to make up the time.''

After his midday meal, instead of retiring to his room for an afternoon of quiet study, Thorolf set out for the consular palace. He had to wait an hour before being admitted to see his father. While he waited, pictures of Yvette floated through his mind. If only old Bardi had not blundered; or if the spell could have been postponed for a single day. . . .

Thorolf had never felt apologetic about his virginal state, since the Paganist religion was fairly strict in its sexual standards. Because of his brawn, none of the soldiers beneath his orders dared to chaff him about it, after he had thrown one scoffer twenty feet into a manure pile. His fellow sergeant, Regin, who notoriously flouted these standards, sometimes remarked after a weekend of revelry:

"Well, Thorolf old boy, hast become a real man yet?''

But he said it in fun. He could do it with impunity because he was Thorolf's closest friend among the soldiers.

At last Thorolf was waved into the Consul's inner

chamber. Clad in official scarlet, Consul Zigram over-
flowed the chair in which he sat behind an oversized
desk. The side of this desk toward the Consul was
curved to make room for Thorolf's father's bulk, which
his luxuriant snow-white beard covered. His golden
chain and medallion of office were hung round his neck
atop the beard, which would otherwise have concealed
them.

"Greetings, son!" puffed the Consul. "How wags
thy world?"

"Well enough, Father. Hast heard of my involvement
with the Countess of Grintz?"

"Only that ye brought this fair fugitive to Vasco's inn
for the night. Where is she now? We lust not for a
confrontation with the Duke of Landai."

"At Bardi's urging, I left her in charge of Doctor
Orlandus, to treat her for an ill. Now I would fain ask
some questions about this Orlandus and his Sophonomists."

The change in the Consul's aspect startled Thorolf.
His fat features seemed to collapse like a ruptured bladder, while his eyes rounded with fear. Casting about
furtive looks, like those of a rabbit stealing cabbages,
he whispered:

"Son, son, mention not that name within these
walls!"

"But Father, these folk might be dangerous to the
Commonwealth! Orlandus' guards go about with swords
unwired, as if members of the army or the Constabulary—"

"Shh!" Zigram laid a finger to his lips. "Not a word
about them or their leader! I cannot explain here, for
the walls have ears."

Thorolf frowned. "As bad as that? Where can we
talk frankly, then? In your private quarters?"

"Nay; I never know when a flunky or chambermaid
hath been suborned."

L. Sprague de Camp & Catherine Crook de Camp

"How about our old house? We could ask the tenants to leave us alone in a room—"

"Nay; knew ye not? The tenant hath bought the place."

"I knew there was talk—" began Thorolf.

"Well, he did. Without your mother, I saw no use in keeping up that old pile, especially since I won the consular election. And speaking of your mother, I never truly appreciated the lass whilst she lived." Zigram hastily wiped a damp eyelid with his sleeve.

Thorolf proposed: "Shall I take a room at Vasco's again? I must return thither to give Vasco a sheet I borrowed."

The Consul hesitated, then said: "Nay, nay; they'd follow me." Still whispering, Zigram added: "My dear son, have nought to do with these folk, any more than you'd pick up a viper with a bare hand! Flee all contact! A clean pair of heels is your only salvation."

"But I cannot abandon the Countess in their custody—"

"A pox upon your Countess! Some decadent aristocrat from the benighted feudal regime of Carinthia—"

Thorolf interrupted: "With all due respect, you know not whereof you speak. You've never seen her. If there be aught Yvette is not, it's decadent."

The consul's white-browed eyes narrowed. "So vehement, stripling? Art in love with the dame?"

"Of course not! After but one day and night—"

"Night, eh? I know these high-born jades. Didst have a good time?"

"Father, you are impossible! I have *not* bedded her—"

"Well, then, do ye court her honorably? Titled wenches make chancy wives, being full of hoity-toity snobbery. They fancy themselves beings of a superior species by virtue of blue blood, when 'tis well known that most noble houses were founded by successful ban-

52

ditti who frightened some weakling ruler into granting titles.''

"She has some of that," Thorolf conceded. "She thinks in the imperative mood. A pity; she's a fascinating creature. But I will do what my conscience commands.''

"From what my spies tell me," said the Consul, "she is a combination of the goddess Rianna and a man-eating tigress.''

"Not so formidable as all that, Father! She's a small person, but with more energy per pound than I've ever seen.''

Zigram mused: "I'm concerned for my line, with mine only son still unwed at nearly thirty. Since high rank in the state be closed to you by our nepotism law, at least whilst I remain in office, ye were better-advised to court the daughter of some banker or rich merchant.''

"And you," said Thorolf, "were better-advised to eat less and exercise more, if you'd fain live through that second term of office you seek." He rose. "Come over to the barracks, and I'll work fifty pounds of that fat off.''

"Speak not rudely to thy sire, boy!''

"Nor you to me. But come, walk with me to the barracks. It will do you good, and we shall be where none can overhear.''

"Oh, very well." With a groan, Zigram heaved himself out of his chair and shrugged a black cloak over his crimson doublet.

In the street, Thorolf gave his father a sharp look. "Tell me, Father, what hold have the Sophonomists on you? For some I'm sure they have, to make a brave man quail at their mere mention.''

"Nay, son; meddle not. 'Twill do you no good.''

"Father, I insist! Have they discovered something to your discredit in your past?''

"Nay, nay; 'tis—a small matter of no import.''

"If it were so little, you'd not flinch at its mere mention. Out with it! If it affects mine own future, I should be forewarned. Am I your son or not?" Thorolf used the tone of a professor to a refractory pupil.

"Oh, very well," said Zigram dejectedly. "They discovered that, years ago whilst your dear mother was yet young, I had taken up with another woman, over in Uberunnen. I had in fact committed bigamy. If the tale were spread abroad, away would go my chances for a second term."

"Ha!" said Thorolf. "And what of this other wench? Meanst that I have a stepmother across the mountains?"

"Nay. She got a quiet annulment and hath since rewed. I've not set eyes upon her for years. But you comprehend the potential scandal. By Kernun's antlers, breathe not a word of this!"

"Never fear. How did they find out? Filching documents?"

"I know not; but I am sure they have done the like with certain senators. Thus grows their power."

"What is this lady's name? I ought to know in case I should encounter her."

"Nay, that I will not tell. Let the dead past . . ."

They argued, but Zigram was adamant. At last Thorolf said: "My Countess brought her coronet with her. Who were the safest banker to leave it with?"

"Waddo Sifson were as good as any."

"Thanks. Here are the barracks. Come over some time and, if you won't take exercises, at least watch me at mine. Good day, sire!"

IV
The Desirable Dragon

During the following days, Thorolf's attention was often distracted by thoughts of Yvette. He saw her fine-boned face in the visage of every girl he passed on the streets. Afternoons, after drill, he found himself lingering on the Street of Clockmakers, ostensibly absorbed in an elaborate astronomical timepiece in a merchant's showcase. By silvered disks, gilded hands, and moving mythological figurines it displayed not only the time but also the phases of the moon, the tides, and the motions of the planets.

Thorolf's examination of the clock was but a pretext for shooting furtive glances up Castle Hill to the fortress where he had left Yvette. He realized that his father was right; he was falling in love.

He knew it was a folly. Yvette had told him plainly that her next husband must be of noble blood, an issue that she took with utmost seriousness; and he was just a plain citizen of the Commonwealth. Even if she accepted, she was too arrogant and aggressive to make an endurable wife. She would insist that he move out of the barracks, buy a house, and hire servants; and away would go whatever money he might still save for his advanced studies.

Her candid confession of unchastity also bothered him. He had long assumed that he would marry a virgin and that they would explore the mysteries of love together. This was still the common, socially accepted pattern of behavior in Rhaetia, where Doctor Mersius' contraceptive spell was not yet widely known. If many Rhaetians failed to live up to it, enough others adhered to it to make such behavior no cause for remark.

Thorolf was not much surprised by Yvette's candid admissions; he had long heard tales of the Carinthian nobility. But even if he overlooked this matter, the straitlaced Zurshnitters were cold to brides with colorful pasts. Marriage to Yvette, even in the wildly improbable case she would have him, had as favorable a prospect as a wrestling match with one of the fifty-foot serpents of Thither Ethiopia.

His first task was to get her away intact, in her proper form. This done, he thought that, from her free-and-easy ways in such matters, she might permit him some nights of lechery despite his lowly social standing on her scale. He avidly desired such a union, however ephemeral. But, inexperienced as he was, he doubted that he could so please her as to change her basic nature, which was too firmly set in the aristocratic mold.

Still, no matter how much he berated himself as a sentimental fool, Thorolf still loitered in the Street of Clockmakers, pretending an avid interest in clocks while stealing sidelong glances at the bodeful battlements above. At the end of a week, he could stand the suspense no longer. He trudged up the path to the castle and told a mailed guard:

"Kindly take a message to Doctor Orlandus. I am

56

Sergeant Thorolf, and I wish to know the state of the patient I left in his care."

When the guard departed, the other guard said: "Bean't ye he who last week brought some gigantical bug to the castle?"

"You may call it that," said Thorolf.

The guard returned, accompanied by a stout, scowling, red-haired man in a red robe. In no ingratiating tones, the redhead said: "Sergeant, the Master remembers you; but he cannot take time from his world-saving work to answer idle queries. Your Countess shall receive you on the day appointed, a sennight hence. Good day, sir."

The man walked away. The sight of smiles on the faces of the two guards infuriated Thorolf; but he held himself in check. A fight would do no good and, more likely, harm. Instead, he bent his steps toward the headquarters building of the Constabulary.

Gray-haired Chief Constable Lodar said: "The reason these wights roam abroad with swords unwired, Sergeant, is that I have a command from above to turn a blind eye to their venial offenses."

"What's 'above'?" demanded Thorolf. "My esteemed father?"

"Now, now, I would not mingle in a family dispute. Let's say that it came from those superior to me in the government."

"Have the Sophonomists infiltrated the Constabulary?"

"Not to my definite knowledge. Suspecting these men of ambitions inconsistent with proper duty, I have rejected applications when I was certain of such affiliation. But I doubt not that we have some amongst us, as a consequence of the death of Master Eberolf."

"What befell him?" asked Thorolf.

The Chief Constable looked about and lowered his voice. "He was a former Sophonomist who turned against the Order. He went about denouncing them and warning of their ambition to seize the rule of Rhaetia. Well, one morn he was found in an alley, strangled. I assigned Constable Hasding to investigate. He said he was making progress; but one day he fell, or was pushed, from high in the Temple of Irpo and slain. I sought the file of information Hasding had gathered on the death of Eberolf; and lo, 'twas missing! I suspect that someone in the corps extracted it. Other papers, too, are not where they should be in the files.''

"If Orlandus be so great a mage," said Thorolf, "what needs he with planting spies in your midst to filch papers? Why could he not effect his desires by spells?''

"Imprimus, I doubt he's so puissant a wizard as he pretends; that tale of having studied the wisdom of the East in Serica is surely false. At the time he claimed to be so occupied, he was a petty thief in Letitia. Secondly, to make doubly sure that he cast no witchery upon us, I caused old Doctor Bardi to set up a protective spell on all the Constabulary, to render us proof against illusions, transformations, demonic possessions, and similar japes.''

"If Orlandus plant spies amongst your men, why canst not do the same with him? His guards are ordinary men, unlike those delta-possessed diaphanes.''

Lodar smiled quietly. "If we had such nameless informers at work, think ye we'd admit to it?''

Acknowledging the hint with a smile and a nod, Thorolf asked: "Hast heard what befell the Countess of Grintz, when at her behest Bardi tried to cast upon her an illusion spell?''

"I heard it made her into an eight-headed dragon; but I set that aside as mere rumor. We have had no reports of such a monster gobbling our citizens; not that some do not deserve that fate. What, then, did happen?''

Thorolf told his tale, adding: "As you see, dear old Bardi's work is not always to be depended upon."

"It seems to have worked for us," said Lodar. "We tested it, importing a wizard from Tzenric to cast the fellest spells in his armory upon Constable Prisco, who had volunteered."

"I'm happy not to have been in Prisco's boots. What befell?"

"The spell shed the wizard's attacks as featly as good plate armor sheds stones. The old fellow may not be so keen as a razor of the best trollish steel; but this time he was in the gold. We've sought to persuade the government to hire a first-rank wizard full-time, to protect us and the army; but the Senate hath balked at the expense."

"Gramercy for your news," said Thorolf. "Methinks I could use such a protective spell for dealing with Sophonomists."

Next day, Thorolf went to Bardi's house. When the last of Bardi's regular patients had departed, Thorolf told the iatromage:

"Doctor, I would that you gave me the same immunity spell that you cast upon the Constabulary. In six days I must needs fetch Yvette from Castle Zurshnitt, and you know what that may entail."

"Dear me!" Bardi mumbled. "I were glad to, my son, at my usual fee; but there's a difficulty."

"What is that?"

"I no longer have the spell to hand. 'Twas from a book—not one of mine, but one in the Horgus College Library. I copied it out on a paper, and anon I stowed this sheet betwixt the pages of one of those." A sweep of Bardi's bony hand indicated the disorderly rows of books on the sagging shelves.

"Well, why can't you simply take it out of the book in question?"

"Alas, I have forgotten which volume I placed it in."

Thorolf counted ten and then spoke with poorly concealed exasperation: "Then tell me which volume in the college library you took it from, and I'll make my own copy."

"Dear, dear, I have forgotten that, too!"

"Well, you can go through every one of your own volumes until you come to it, can you not?"

"But that would waste days, and I could not afford the time, with the rent due in a week. Let me be for a few days; the title of one book or t'other will surely pop into mind."

Thorolf sighed. "Oh, well, let's go to dinner at Vasco's."

"Gramercy, albeit ye must not detain me there overlong. There is some reason why I must return to my house this even, but I cannot recall what it is."

"Ere we go," said Thorolf, "make sure your head be securely fastened, lest you forget it."

As they entered the Green Dragon, Vasco said: "Sergeant Thorolf, some men were here asking after you this afternoon."

"What sort of men?"

"Six or seven, clad as traveling merchants; but beneath their outer garments I espied the gleam of mail. The sword one wore was long enough to expose the chape below the hem of's cloak. They also inquired after your Countess."

"What did you tell them?"

"That I'd seen neither hide nor hair of you, or the Countess either, for above a sennight."

Thorolf exchanged glances with Bardi. "Did their speech betray their origin?"

Vasco chewed his lip before answering. "Meseems their speech bore the soft accents of Carinthia, albeit I'm no savant in such matters."

"Duke Gondomar's men, or I'm a Saracen," muttered Thorolf. To the innkeeper he said: "What is your choicest tonight, Vasco?"

At table, Thorolf discussed Duke Gondomar's persistent efforts to recapture his recreant betrothed. Bardi said: "If another magical menace threatened you, I might do something to protect you; but I am long past the age for swordplay. Belike ye could persuade a stout comrade-in-arms to accompany you in the city streets."

Back at Bardi's house, Thorolf was watching the iatromage putter among his books and paraphernalia when a fist assaulted the door.

"Oh, dear me!" exclaimed Bardi. "What I had forgot was that the Executive Committee of the Magical Guild meets here tonight."

"Who are they?"

"There's Sordamor, the Chief Executive Officer; he's the showy one. There's Gant, the drug-ridden one, who looks like a disheveled crow. And there's that smiling little villain Avain, our treasurer. But ye are not supposed to be here!" Bardi looked around. "Hide behind the curtain in yon alcove, and yarely!"

The alcove was dark save for the pale sheet of light that came through the crack in the curtain. Thorolf had to force himself in, since he had a buried fear of dark enclosures. When the soldier's eyes adjusted to the gloom, he looked around and almost jumped out of his skin. On a shelf at the back of the alcove, silhouetted against the oiled-paper window, crouched an enormous spider, with a body the size of Thorolf's two fists and hairy legs an ell in length.

Thorolf had snatched out his dagger when the sound of persons entering the sanctum made him freeze, glaring at the spider. It reminded him of the giant arachnids, with bodies the size of casks, said to dwell in the Forest of Bricken.

When the spider on the shelf remained immobile, Thorolf essayed a cautious approach and observed no response. Eventually, by touching one of the legs with the point of his knife, he satisfied himself that what he saw was either a dead spider mounted by a taxidermist or a statue.

He put his eye to the crack between the curtains. Three of Bardi's fellow magicians were taking seats while Bardi set out goblets and a bottle. Thorolf surveyed the Executive Committee.

The tall, thin, shabby man who faced him must, he thought, be Gant the drug addict. His garb was that of a common workman: a rusty black tunic and hose beneath a shapeless black hat. The fellow might have been a grave digger—or, from his unnatural pallor, one of a grave digger's clients.

Seated in profile to Thorolf was a big, handsome, clean-shaven man in gaudy raiment. Thorolf knew him by sight as Sordamor, who collected the fattest fees of any magician in Zurshnitt. His hose bore loud checkered patterns, red and black on one leg and yellow and blue on the other. When he moved his head, the jewels in his emerald earrings winked in the lamplight.

By elimination, the remaining mage, facing Sordamor, must be Avain. He was older than the other two but younger than Bardi; short, bald, rotund, and radiating bluff honesty and sterling worth.

Bardi pulled the cork and poured. As they solemnly took their first sips, their host asked: "Well, Sordamor?"

"Marvelous!" said the loudly clad man. "Whence gat ye it?"

"From Kolos, in the Helladic Isles."

Thorolf's nose felt out of joint. During all his many visits to the iatromage's sanctum, Bardi had never offered him a treat of this rare vintage. Evidently it was saved for Bardi's fellow wizards.

The meeting was called to order. After tedious organizational preliminaries—reading minutes, listening to the report of Avain as treasurer—the four engaged in a long wrangle over admission of one Alberic, a magician recently settled in Zurshnitt after fleeing persecution in Locania.

"First thing ye know," said Bardi, "every one of these damned Locanian refugees will wish to join, even if they command spells no more puissant than one for finding a lost penny. Is competition not severe enough already?"

"But if we admit them not," said Avain, "soon or late they'll assemble to form their own rival guild."

" 'Twere not legal," protested Gant.

"Not now, true," said Avain. "But in concert they can suborn—or convert, if ye prefer—sufficient senators to force a change in the law, to recognize them as a legitimate guild."

"If we admit a horde of Locanians," mused Sordamor, "we shall be hard put to it to keep out Orlandus and his minions. I shudder at that prospect. If we flatly refuse him, he'll act like the bad fairy who wasn't bid to the naming of the royal infant."

"Ye, my friend," said Avain, "have a phobia anent Master Orlandus. Methinks he'd be an ornament to our assembly."

"An ornament who'd soon control us all, as a puppeteer governs his marionettes on strings," croaked Gant. "He's a man of infinite ambition, not a magician of the first rank, and of no character whatsoever. His second, that ruffian Parthenius, is no magician at all but a mere bully-rook without a single familiar at his beck."

Bardi wheezed: "In my judgment, Orlandus began as a mere mundane mountebank, who added a few sleights of true magic to's repertory. Then he found he could make a fortune by peddling a fantastical tale. According to this, supposed to be known only by holders of his bogus advanced degrees, a million million years ago the body his soul then indwelt witnessed the destruction of reptilian man by the evil wizard Zong. A few million years later, Orlandus, in another incarnation, by a mighty spell caused the homeless spirits of these massacred folk to be incarnated in apes, of whom we are the descendants. For aught I know, he may have told that silly tale so oft that he's come to believe it himself.''

Sordamor added: ''From what I hear, Orlandus is somewhat of an idealist in his own ominous way. Since he thinks he knows what is best for all human beings, it's but right that he should become their universal, absolute ruler, to lead them whither they should go.''

''Anyone can rob or murder and claim he did it for idealistic reasons,'' snorted Bardi.

''I'm sure Parthenius, at least, be no idealist,'' growled Gant, ''but a common, sensual mundane, out for what he can get by force or fraud. . . .''

The argument went round and round inconclusively. Then ensued a discussion of Sordamor's project, to offer an annual prize, a golden medal, for the wizard who made the year's outstanding magical advance. A wrangle over a proposal to establish a class of associate membership followed, and then a discussion of whether to raise dues.

This in turn was succeeded by a proposal to hold a magical convention in Zurshnitt, inviting wizards from near and far. All favored the idea enthusiastically until it came to apportioning the actual work of organizing, soliciting, contracting, publishing, and record-keeping. Then each magus proved too busy, or too infirm, or too often out of town to do the task justice. Bardi finally said:

''Let us push off these tasks on our younger members, who'll embrace them as a chance to inflate their self-importance.''

After three hours the meeting broke up. Nothing much had been decided save to place Alberic's application for membership before the next general meeting. When Bardi, having dismissed his guests, flung back the curtains before the alcove, he found Thorolf sitting on the floor with his back to the wall and sound asleep.

Six days later, Thorolf again approached the gate on Castle Hill. This time a gate guard said: "Master Thorolf Zigramson? Ye are expected. Pray wait here."

After a wait, the scarlet-robed, gold-capped person of Orlandus appeared. Smiling broadly, the Psychomage came up to Thorolf and warmly grasped his hand, cooing: "Thrice welcome, dear friend! You will be happy to hear that the lady be wholly restored. Hast the promised sum?"

Thorolf produced a heavy bag of coin and handed it over. Orlandus hefted the bag and tossed it to a guard. "Give this to Master Cadolant to count." He turned back to the gate and called: "Lady Yvette!"

The Countess appeared from the far end of the gate passage; Thorolf thought that she must have been standing just out of sight inside the gate, awaiting Orlandus' call. Thorolf's eyes widened. Instead of the peasant blouse and skirt given her by the smith, she now wore a dove-gray cloak over a golden gown of ladylike quality. A little round azure bonnet topped her golden hair, and her feet were clad in silken slippers suitable for a ballroom. Thorolf cast a questioning glance at Orlandus, who purred:

"Certes, good my Sergeant, you cannot expect me to turn my choicest diaphane out into the rough, rude world appearing like unto a beggar lass, now could you? It is a matter of honor. The cost shall come out of the emolument from Doctor Bardi and your esteemed self."

"But . . ." said Thorolf, nonplussed. "I understood . . ."

"That I should keep her locked up here until the last penny were paid? Not so. She'll gladly go forth with her trusty friend and come back hither in due course. Won't you, my dear?" he added, turning toward Yvette.

"Yea, Master," she replied in a level, expressionless

voice, like someone speaking an unfamiliar language. "Hail, Sergeant Thorolf! Wouldst care to show me the sights of Zurshnitt?"

"I shall be delighted," said Thorolf, bowing but with a tinge of uncertainty in his voice. Her blank, expressionless stare and flat monotone were utterly unlike the vivacious, expressive, self-assertive Yvette whom he had brought to Zurshnitt. This, he thought, deserved investigation; but it would not do to betray his suspicions now.

"Sergeant!" said Orlandus crisply, "methought you'd have a carriage for her. Those silken shoon will not long endure the cobbles."

"I expected not—" began Thorolf.

"You thought she'd remain mewed up? A trivial misunderstanding. Since 'tis partly my fault, I'll lend mine own carriage, freshly imported from Sogambrium. When she return hither, you will I am sure provide suitable transport."

He turned to command a gate guard. Presently a brougham, black with a golden coat of arms on either side, drawn by a pair of matched blacks and driven by a yellow-robed coachman, trotted out from behind the keep. With a charming smile, Orlandus said to Thorolf:

"You must return to visit. We shall have much to say to each other."

As the vehicle, with the coachman straining at the brake, inched its way down the winding road on the far side of Castle Hill, Thorolf examined the conveyance with interest. It was his first ride in such a carriage, of which there were only a few in Zurshnitt. These vehicles had come into vogue a few decades before among the nobility and the richer merchants. Owners of these newfangled conveyances at once began pestering their governments for improvements in streets and roads, to let them travel more comfortably than on the back of horse or mule, in horse litters, or in farm carts. One could now go by carriage all the way from Zurshnitt to Sogambrium or Letitia.

Thorolf spent the rest of the day in giving Yvette a tour of the Rhaetian capital, explaining its sights and monuments: "Now that, Countess, is a statue of our great patriot, Arnalt of Thessen, who routed the Carinthians at Gorbec and so laid the foundations of our Commonwealth. . . ."

"What is that?" asked Yvette, pointing to what looked like a large animal covered with tawny-yellow fur, lying in a gutter.

Delighted to see his love show a spark of interest in anything, Thorolf replied: "That's a troll. Methought you knew about them."

"I had never seen one. Is it alive?"

"Aye; you can see its ribs move. Probably sleeping off a debauch. A few dwell in the city, doing menial work requiring great strength; but when paid off they drink themselves fap."

"I see," she said, relapsing into her former state. To Thorolf's further expositions she answered only: "Yea, Sergeant," in a leaden monotone. Thorolf felt he was showing the town to an utter stranger inhabiting Yvette's fetching body. Moreover, this stranger had no interest in the sights of Zurshnitt. At last he said:

"My dear, yonder lies the famous Zoölogical Park of Zurshnitt. Wouldst care for a stroll therein?"

"Aye, Sergeant, if you wish." She looked at her feet. "But these light shoon are unsuited to walking. Couldst purchase me a pair of stout overshoes?"

"Hm. No shoemaker could make us a pair whilst we wait. But— I have it! There's a shop run by high-born ladies for charitable purposes. People give it their used goods, which the ladies sell cheaply and devote the money to good works. They may have a pair that would fit."

* * *

An hour later they descended from the carriage at the entrance to the zoo, with Yvette more substantially shod. Thorolf told the driver to wait, paid the admission fee, and escorted Yvette in.

"Now these," he explained, pointing to a group of huge, black, long-horned bovines, "are aurochs from the Vilitzian Forest, in the northern marches of the Empire. Albeit they resemble our domestic cattle, they are fierce and untamable. Over here is a unicorn from the Forest of Bricken, now a rare species." The mouse-brown beast indicated, munching hay and browse, was the size of a buffalo but of more porcine appearance. Its huge head was decorated with bony bumps and a spirally twisted single horn.

They moved on to the next enclosure, in which lay a large, pallid reptile, like a long-legged crocodile, covered with short hairlike bristles. The animal sprawled immobile with closed eyes, only an occasional movement of its rib cage indicating life.

"That," said Thorolf, "is the Helvetian mountain dragon. There are still a few up in the troll country."

For once Yvette said something other than "Yea, Sergeant." She replied: "Aye, Master Thorolf. The Emperor hath a similar beast from Pathenia in his menagerie in Sogambrium."

"How looked it, Countess?"

"Much like yon reptile, save without the bristles and of a darker hue. As with other reptiles, the sight thereof provides but a minimum of enchantment, as it lies all day without moving a whisker. Since the day wanes, should you not proceed to your inn? A repast were welcome."

"A splendiferous idea! The park will soon close anyway. Let's back to the carriage."

As they turned away from the dragon's enclosure, Thorolf found himself confronting a group of men. There were seven, in the sober dress of traveling merchants, but strapping fellows who bore themselves like soldiers. One stepped forward. "Sergeant Thorolf, methinks?"

Thorolf bristled; these were probably the men who had sought him at the Green Dragon and therefore henchmen of the Duke of Landai. "And what if I be?" he said, sliding a hand toward his hilt. As a soldier of his rank on active service, Thorolf was not required to immobilize his blade with peace wires.

"My good sir," said the man, "we have a proposal that, of a surety, will capture your interest." The man made a gesture. Two of the group skirted around Thorolf and Yvette and leaped the low fence about the dragon's enclosure. Thorolf, fearing attack from behind, whirled in time to see one of the twain wrench open the cage door, while the other whirled a sling he took from beneath his clothes.

"Ho there!" shouted Thorolf. "Are you mad?"

The leaden sling bullet struck the mountain dragon in the ribs with a solid thump. The big emerald eyes snapped open; up came the fanged head. The dragon lurched to its feet and started for the open door. From its gaping jaws came a long, groaning bellow. The two who had aroused it ran.

Other visitors shrieked and stampeded away from the dragon's cage. Behind him, Thorolf heard a scream in Yvette's familiar soprano. Turning again, he saw two other pseudo-merchants dragging her off. She struggled, but the men easily bore the slight woman away. Behind Thorolf, the dragon roared as it emerged.

As the spectators fled, keepers converged on the site, shouting questions and demands. Two dragged up a large net, which they threw over the dragon's head and forequarters. Another struck one of the men dragging Yvette with a quarterstaff. Staggered, the abductor released Yvette's arm, whereupon the Countess kicked the other kidnapper in the crotch.

"She-devil!" yelled the man, clutching his affected parts.

Trying to hasten to Yvette with drawn sword, Thorolf found his way blocked by a cluster of zookeepers, one of whom cried: "Seize him! 'Tis he who enlarged the dragon!"

"Fools!" shouted Thorolf. "Yon runagates loosed the beast, to kidnap the lady—"

He tried to push past the keepers; but they closed ranks before him. When one grabbed him, he knocked the man down with his free hand; but another threw a net over him. It was smaller than the net in which the dragon now struggled, writhed, and snapped but quite as effective in immobilizing its victim.

"Yvette!" yelled Thorolf. "Tell these idiots who I am!"

Mechanically she recited: "He is Sergeant Thorolf of the Fourth Rhaetian Foot."

"We care not if he be a general!" a keeper cried. "No man shall molest our animals!"

"Hold! What's all this?" demanded a new voice, that of a lean, gray-haired man. Thorolf recognized Berthar, the director of the Zoölogical Park. He and the keepers all broke into heated explanations at once, while Yvette stood silently.

"Release Sergeant Thorolf!" said Berthar. "I know him for a true man. Ye say a gang of ready-for-aughts sought to abduct this lady? Where are they now?"

"They vanished whilst your men were netting me," Thorolf spat.

"We shall sift this matter. But excuse me; I must see that our dragon be well encaged."

When the hubbub had died, Thorolf took Yvette to Berthar's chamber of office. The room had books and papers piled on every horizontal surface, even the floor. Some of the piles were topped by the skulls of beasts that had dwelt and died in the park. A corner was occupied by a glass-paned terrarium.

Berthar waved his visitors to chairs and poured small

goblets of wine. After Thorolf had told of the pursuit of Yvette by Duke Gondomar, Berthar said:

"I shall alert the Constabulary to watch for these rogues."

"I've already told Lodar," said Thorolf, "but an additional reminder were not amiss."

"Is the Countess hale?" asked Berthar, nodding toward the silent Yvette. "She seems as quiet as Arnalt's tomb."

Thorolf shrugged. "Unharmed in body; but she is under certain—ah—influences. How have you been, Berthar?"

The Director spread his hands. "Nigh nibbled to death by the ducks of daily life. It hath been so ever since my former wife ran off with that water-of-life salesman. Today, for ensample, within a few hours, our Pantorozian tiger died; a keeper succumbed to the delusion that he was a Mauretanian viper and went about wriggling on his belly and trying to bite people; and Banker Gallus demanded that I give his old horse a good home, albeit without providing funds to do so. Then, to cap it all, came the raid of those rogues who were fain to enlarge the dragon, I ween to furnish a diversion to cover their abduction of your lady."

Thorolf noted: "I do perceive that your post be not one for weaklings. How flourishes the park?"

The Director shrugged. "As usual. It were a dire calamity had our prize specimen escaped. Obeying its natural instincts, it would have snapped up a tasty citizen or two. Then nought would have dissuaded your thick-skulled military from slaying the beast, as if one mountain dragon were not worth a score of human beings."

Thorolf raised his eyebrows. "How reckon you that?"

"The mountain dragon is an endangered species, whereas the world swarms with humanity. Man is in no danger of extermination, unless it destroy itself by devilish novel weapons like those Serican thunder tubes I hear of. It would serve the species right.''

Thorolf gave a quiet laugh. "I never thought of it thus. Doubtless being human has warped my thinking.''

"No species outranks any other in the eyes of the gods!" Berthar leaned forward. "Thorolf, know ye that I have a special fund for the acquisition of rare specimens, from donations by some wealthy citizens? Could I but obtain a female mountain dragon, 'twere worth ten thousand marks to its captor.''

Thorolf whistled. "A lot of money for one stupid, dangerous beast!''

"My great ambition is to breed the creatures, and our lone specimen is a male." Glancing at the closed door, the director lowered his voice. "I have a personal reason to boot. I have long been an active alumnus of Horgus College. My banker friends tell me that, an I can bring off this feat, they'll see me elected to the Board.''

"Alas!" said Thorolf. "I fear my soldierly duties leave me little time for dragon hunting. Anyway, how should I know a female dragon? How does one tell?''

"The female lacks the crest and the hornlike knobs above the eyes of the male. Some still roam the higher ranges, in trollish territory. Here, let me give you a copy of my monograph on the beast. I plan a journey into mountain-dragon land, if I can get the trolls' permission.''

"Thanks. To hunt your dragon?''

"Nay; for that I lack the means. 'Twould need a numerous party, sure to arouse the trolls' suspicion. What I seek is less formidable.'' He pointed to the terrarium.

Thorolf bent over the glass enclosure, seeing a surface of pebbles, sand, and moss, with water at one end. In the water a finger-long black newt with red spots on its hide moved slowly about with languid waves of its tail.

"What's that?" asked Thorolf. "Some kind of lizard?"

"Nay; a salamander of a kind hitherto unreported from Rhaetia."

"What's the difference?"

"Lizards live wholly on land, whereas salamanders are hatched in water, like tadpoles, and dwell both in water and on land. The great Doctor Karlovius at Saalingen, who reduced the chaos of the animal world to orderly families, genera, and species, hath made the distinction clear. I seek additional samples; less impressive than a dragon, belike, but not without significance in the heavenly scheme. If it differ sufficiently from the lowland type, I may have an unreported new species. Meanwhile, I pray, bear my dragon offer in mind."

"I shall, if I ever return to academe."

"I've heard of your scholarly troubles. Couldst not apply to some other center of learning?"

"So I did; but each demanded my scholarly records. Then they wrote to Horgus, and the replies they gat did damn me." He rose. "Thanks for the drink. My lady hungers, so we shall be off."

Thorolf took Yvette to the Green Dragon Inn and sent Orlandus' carriage and driver away. Yvette limped slightly as they entered the inn. To Thorolf's question she replied:

"I hurt my toe when I kicked that scrowle in's manhood. These shoon you bought me were too light for such footballery; next time I shall wear mountaineer's boots."

Thorolf asked Vasco if the room they had occupied before was vacant and engaged it for the night. Yvette stood silently by. Vasco gave the couple a sharp look, suppressed a smile, and handed Thorolf the key. "Wilt sup here, Sergeant?"

"Aye," Thorolf said. In the common room, Thorolf

hung Yvette's gray cloak on a peg and held a chair for her. He almost whistled at the sight of the costly golden gown. It was a shimmery beaded affair, far too dressy for Vasco's, which was largely frequented by salesmen for Zurshnitt's far-famed clocks and cutlery. A large ruby brooch glittered between her small breasts; Thorolf could only guess that the diamonds around it were genuine.

Thorolf ordered a bottle of Vasco's best wine and then dinner. This time, she lagged behind him in drinking, while he watched her sharply. When he had drunk enough to feel the effects, he reasoned that, since he outweighed her two to one, she ought by now to be thoroughly besotted. Perhaps, he thought, the wine would subdue whatever entity had taken possession of her being and allow her natural self to break through. But, although she drank almost as much as he, she showed no effect whatever.

Through the repast, Thorolf kept up a running chatter, trying to elicit human reactions from Yvette. He told tales from Rhaetian history and legend; she merely nodded and said: "Yea, I understand." He told jokes, to which she smiled politely but without mirth. He made up versicles:

"If Rhaetia lacks nobles, we've many skilled workers.
        We've craftsmen and merchants and soldiers in
        plenty,
        And clockmakers, herdsmen; of bankers there's
        twenty.
Amid all this bustle, there's no room for shirkers!
But if you disdain our prosaical nation,
        And if you crave troubadours, poets, or knights,
        Or gallants and other romantical wights,
You'd better look elsewhere for gratification!"

He even told jokes of the randy sort favored in barracks; which, being a prim Rhaetian at heart, he would not ordinarily have uttered in the hearing of a lady. Still she only smiled politely.

This, Thorolf decided, was a waste of time. Instead, he began questioning: "Tell me where you are quartered."

"In one of the little rooms on the second level, for advanced diaphanes," she said.

"Where are those cubicles? I've but once set foot in the castle."

"When erst you brought me thither, you ascended a stair and turned right to the Chamber of Audience, didst not?"

"Aye."

"Well, you must needs turn left at the top of the stairs instead and pass a row of chambers betwixt the left-side corridor and the outer wall. Mine is the second from the stair end."

"Couldst draw me a plan?" asked Thorolf, taking notepad and writing materials from his scrip.

"Nay; but if you will draw, I'll correct your sketch."

Soon, with some spillage of ink, Thorolf had a ragged plan of the second storey of the keep. He asked: "Hast a room to yourself?"

"Aye."

"Do you always sleep alone, or does Orlandus—ah . . ."

"Nay; the charms of women's bodies beguile him not. Once he caught a guard sneaking into my chamber, hoping for a speedy lectual canter. The master had the fellow dragged away by male diaphanes."

"What befell the would-be lecher?"

"I know not; but later that night I heard masculine screams."

Thorolf changed the subject. "Now tell me what you do during the day—any ordinary day."

"We rise early to break our fast. Then the Master hath assigned me to the Record Room, where we keep files on Sophonomy's foes. 'Tis not so different from what my confidential clerk did when I ruled in Grintz. Each bit of news of the scoundrels is pricked down and placed in a folder. The folders stand in alphabetical order.''

"Where is this Record Room?" asked Thorolf. He had visions of abstracting his father's dossier and thus breaking the Sophonomists' hold on the Consul.

" 'Tis in the crypt below the castle, directly beneath my sleeping chamber. The area combines two of the cells of the dungeon. The Master had the wall betwixt them knocked down and the room aired and scrubbed. 'Twere no bad place to work, save for the plaints and the rattling of chains of the prisoners in the other cells.''

"Prisoners?" Thorolf came alert. "Whom, pray, does your Master confine against their will?''

"They are all probationers who have committed grave offenses. Not common, mundane Rhaetian citizens, if that concern you.''

Thorolf filed the information for possible future use against the cult. When the repast was over, Thorolf led Yvette unresisting up the stair to the same handsomely furnished room. Inside, she said:

"I do recall this chamber, where you and I once attempted a night of pleasure—oh, it must be half a month agone. My memory thereof wavers phantasmally; I have a dream of living as some sort of devil-fish. Where sat we when something went amiss?''

Thorolf said: "I was on yonder settee, and you were giving me lessons in kissing.'' His heart thudded.

"Excellent! Seat yourself, Sergeant, and we shall resume where we left off.''

She pushed him back until he sat down. Then pirouetting slowly, she shed the shimmering golden gown. The fine linen shift beneath it followed as she pulled it off a finger's length at a time, like a skillful courtesan arousing her client. She sat down on Thorolf's lap and kissed him until the blood pounded in his ears. The air was redolent of a costly perfume.

She stood up and stepped back, glancing at the vacated lap. "Art ready?"

"Aye," he said thickly, wondering how he could stand up while still clad.

"Then you shall have your desire once a small matter hath been attended to." Her tone became as briskly businesslike as that of a Rhaetian banker.

"Eh? What's this?"

From her reticule Yvette brought out a sheet of paper, folded and refolded into a small packet. She spread the paper on the writing desk, saying: "You have but to sign this trivial engagement, and my body shall be yours. Here's pen and ink—and one thing more!"

She picked up the golden dress and detached the ruby brooch. "When you sign, I shall prick your thumb and press it to the contract."

"Damn!" muttered Thorolf. "Every time we . . ." His irritation turned to ire. "Why on earth should I drip blood on this paper?"

"The Master insists. It validates the contract."

For a heartbeat, Thorolf's passion pulled him forward while his prudence held him back. Then he growled: "I'll sign nought without reading it first."

He settled himself on the writing chair and moved the candle closer to the paper. He read that the signer bound himself to apply for membership in Sophonomy, to enroll in the prescribed courses, diligently to pursue these studies for the glory of Sophonomy and the benefit of mankind, and to pay the required fees.

Thorolf looked narrowly at Yvette. She was still a gorgeous creature, but this crass and ominous bargain chilled his lust. That drop of blood would likely give Orlandus some magical hold upon him; if he displeased the Master, he, too, might be turned into an octopus.

"What is the purpose of this document?" he asked, keeping his voice emotionless.

"To do the Master's will. I know no details; I do but know: no contract, no venery. Come, Sergeant, wouldst not show yourself as proficient at this kind of riding as that upon your mighty steed?'' She leaned over and began plucking at his ties, laces, and buttons, rubbing a small but firm breast against his cheek.

It revolted Thorolf that Orlandus' magic had reduced this queenly woman to a kind of fancy whoredom. Be crafty! he commanded himself as he turned away from the desk, saying:

''Yvette, my dear, this contract is a serious matter. I must think ere deciding.'' He stepped to the door. ''I shall go for a walk in the night air. Wait not upon my return, but go to bed when you list.''

''But—''

''If upon my return I have decided to sign, I shall rouse you. Good night!''

V
Maleficent Murder

          In the fading twilight, Thorolf strode briskly to Bardi's house. When the soldier had told his tale, Bardi fingered his straggling beard and mused: "My congratulations, Thorolf, on your self-restraint. Few stout fellows of your age would have shown the like."

"Hardest damned 'nay' I ever said in my life," grunted Thorolf.

"As for your lady, it sounds to me as if she were possessed by a delta. She is what the country folk call 'pixilated.' Were I seeking a woman, an unlikely thing at my age—" Bardi gave a dry chuckle. "—I should choose one less prone to magical misfortunes."

"Some of which you yourself brought about," grumped Thorolf. "And just what, pray, is a delta?"

"A delta is one of the inhabitants of the spirit world. Members of this species are invisible on this plane, save that in the dark you can see one as a point of twinkling light. Also, a skilled sorcerer can capture it, force it into this world, and compel it to occupy the body of a human being.''

''Wouldst call that diabolic possession?''

''Not exactly, nay. Deltas are not evil spirits; they have no special bent toward inflicting weal or woe upon us mortals. They are not highly intelligent and, when controlled by a wizard, obey the commands of him who captures them, like well-trained dogs. Thus they compel the bodies they possess to do as the magus orders. But I must see your lady with mine own eyes.''

''Come, then.'' As they walked toward the Green Dragon, Thorolf asked: ''How complete is the sorcerer's domination? Will a delta-possessed victim slay him or herself at the mage's command?''

''I know not for certain,'' said Bardi. ''Methinks it doth depend upon two factors: the servility of the delta toward the mage and the strength of mind of the victim. These factors vary. I have heard that, when the sorcerer gives the delta a command that violates the most fervent conviction of the possessed one, the subject's body is frozen to immobility. Pray slow down, Thorolf,'' he puffed. ''Mine aged limbs are not up to your soldiery stride!''

At the Green Dragon, Thorolf found the chamber feebly lit by a single candle and Yvette asleep in the bed. Upon the arrival of Thorolf and Bardi, she awoke and sat up, the blanket and sheet falling away from her slender torso.

''Sergeant,'' she asked in her leaden monotone, ''who is this man?''

''You've met Doctor Bardi, Yvette,'' said Thorolf. ''Remember that we sought out Doctor Bardi when you wished to change your appearance to foil pursuers?''

She shook her head. ''It is all confused. But what brings him hither? Would he bed me, also? I am not empowered to grant—''

"Thankee for the compliment," murmured Bardi. "But—"

"Nay, nay!" Thorolf interposed hastily. "He would merely verify your health."

"My health is excellent," she said. "If he fear injury from your great—"

"Nought like that, my dear," Thorolf interrupted. "Do but sit you quiet for a moment!"

Bardi changed his eyeglasses, lit another candle, and held it close to Yvette while studying her eyes and looking down her throat. Then he set down the candle.

"Wilt see me safely home, Thorolf?" he asked. "I am too old and frail to wander the nighted streets alone, with ruffians aprowl. But pray, run not mine old legs off!"

"Certes," said Thorolf. "I shall soon return, Yvette. Go back to sleep, my dear."

As he and the ancient mage traversed the darkened streets, Thorolf said: "Well, Doctor, what thinkst?"

"Meseems a plain case of delta possession."

"Can this spirit be exorcised?"

"Not by me, and mayhap not even by Orlandus, who placed it there. Betimes the deltas come to enjoy residing in a mortal frame and refuse to vacate, like mundane tenants who fall behind with their rent. Perchance Magus Myrdhin in Kymri or Archmage Valentius in Aemilia could force the interloper out."

"Is it not illegal so to possess another?"

"Aye, aye; it's one of the worst forms of magical malpractice. But ye know as well as I that dark deeds are done even in our law-abiding land. It were hard to assemble evidence that would stand the test in court, even could we discover jurymen not so terrified of sorcerers as to refuse to convict.

"Moreover, our public prosecutors dislike cases involving magic. To forestall employment of spells to subvert justice, the prosecutor must either hire a rival wizard, at public expense, to guard the court by counterspells; or bind and gag the magician, leaving but one of's hands unbound to write his answers.''

"Would Orlandus banish the delta when we have paid all of his bill?" asked Thorolf hopefully.

"Count not upon it. His diaphanes are the primary tools wherewith he hopes to further his ambitions; so why should he yield up one?''

"We ought to have been more careful in making an agreement with him.''

"No doubt; but we were under emergent pressure and could not afford lengthy negotiations. Besides, paper promises are still paper promises, which the promiser may break unless the promisee have some exigent hold upon him.''

"Such, say, as a hostage?''

"Aye.'' Bardi fingered his straggly beard. "As things do stand, the only sure release of these deltas back to their native plane is the death of him who installed them. Then, soon or late, they quit the bodies thus possessed and retreat to their proper sphere. I ween they wax homesick.''

Thorolf frowned. "To slay the Psychomage were a large order, to say nought of the law I've sworn to uphold.''

"Oh, my dear Sergeant, think not of such a foray! Orlandus will anticipate your assault and, though he be not a wizard to the highest class, will ready a lethal defense.''

"Then how to rescue the lady? Could I not seek magical aid of mine own?''

Bardi spread his hands helplessly. "I were as useless against him as a fly whisk against a dragon.''

"Who, then?''

"Dear me! I know not who might better serve your turn. Sordamor would charge an emperor's ransom; Gant hath been effective but is now enslaved by his drug; Avain is a treacherous rascal.''

"That smiling little man?"

"Yea verily. As the playwright Helmanax wrote, a man can smile and smile and still be a scoundrel."

Thorolf pondered, his worried thoughts flitting back to the Green Dragon. As they reached the wizard's house, he asked: "Doctor, may I catch a night's sleep here, instead of returning to the inn?"

"Assuredly. But wherefore, with the Queen of the Fays awaiting you in bed?"

"That's just the trouble. Were I alone with her again, I might be more than tempted to sign that cursèd document. I'm in love with the woman she was, so I trust not my resistance. I refused her once, but 'twas a damned near thing."

"With your muscle, she could hardly deny you if you employed force."

"Not my wonted way; and if I did, what then? She said she'd stab any wight who so used her in's sleep. I doubt not that her delta be under orders to do the like."

"Well, use yonder couch if ye like." Bardi fingered his whiskers. "There's something I did mean to tell you, but I've forgotten what. A moment . . ." The wrinkled face cleared. "Ah, yea! I found the book wherein I stowed my notes on the learned Doctor Fausto's volume, *Of the Unrigging of Illusions*. I bethought me yestereve, and by good hap I've bought a phial of Fausto's formula from the apothecary. Bide ye in yon chair for the nonce."

As he rummaged, the magician continued: "Know, Thorolf, that spells fall into two classes: illusory and substantive. Illusory spells do but alter the appearance of things, *exempli gratia* the cheaper spell I offered to put upon the Countess, to make her seem a short, dark, dumpy woman. Such spells are relatively simple.

"Substantive spells, on t'other hand, cause actual re-arrangement of the atoms whereof the thing or person be constructed. . . ."

He droned on about the rival theories of the *modus*

operandi of spells. Then, "Ah, here it is!" He pulled out an ancient codex with a cracked and grimy cover of gilded red leather. Presently Bardi presented Thorolf with a pill and a cupful of water. "Wash it down!" he commanded.

While Thorolf obeyed, Bardi grasped a piece of charcoal and, stooping, marked a small pentacle on the floor. He made a few passes and chanted verses in an unknown tongue. "How feel ye, Sergeant?"

"I tingle all over," said Thorolf. "A slight headache, as if my skull were pressing on my brain."

"That is normal; it will pass."

"I hope this turn me not into some lower form of life!"

"Never fear! I have taken precautions against such an error."

"Is there any way to test the spell?"

"Aye; I'll summon an illusion, and ye shall see how it works."

Bardi lit four black candles and set them in candlesticks on the floor, where they burned with a sinister greenish light. He went through a magical procedure, with words and gestures, causing smokes of magenta, turquoise, and lemon green to rise from the candles. When at last he clapped his hands, the smokes coalesced into a big, black-maned lion, which twitched its tail and gave a hollow roar. Thorolf started back and reached for his sword.

"Do but look closely," said Bardi.

The young man became aware that this lion was transparent; he could see a couple of candleflames through it. He said:

"I understand now, Doctor. How long might this spell last?"

Bardi clapped his hands and uttered a word; the lion faded back into smoke. He gathered and snuffed the candles, saying:

"Belike a month; then it needs renewal. Time was

when I had to crush and mix the ingredients of that pill myself, and a tedious business it was. Now I need but call at the shop of Frigered the Apothecary, where I can purchase many magical preparations made up in pills and drops.''

Thorolf said: ''When I studied at Genuvia, a professor of natural philosophy said that men were working on simpler forms of spells. Instead of all the complications of pentacles, invocations, gestures, and smokes, the complete spell would be contained in a pill, dispensed by an apothecary. This anti-illusion spell, meseems, is a step thither.''

''I've heard such rumors,'' grumbled Bardi, ''but I do not believe 'twill ever come to that. If it be ever reduced to ready-made pills and powders, it will be time for me to take down my sign and retire.''

''Why? You could still sell the pills and powders.''

''So can any man with wit to read a formula and keep his stock in order.''

''So he won't mistakenly turn his client into a tentacled sea monster?'' said Thorolf with a grin.

''Nasty, nasty!'' Bardi wagged a bony forefinger. ''But if all my special skills and knowledge were wasted, I should become a mere file clerk.''

''You could learn the new—''

''My son, there comes a time when one is just too old and tired to cram new skills into one's aged skull.'' Bardi rapped his scalp with his knuckles. ''At any rate, methinks those Serican tubes whereof I hear will put many of my colleagues out of business, since one discharge can wreak more woe in the blink of an eye than a wizard can work with a month of spells.''

''What about your fee? Orlandus will have beggared us by the time he's through.''

Bardi waved a hand. ''Since he hath forced us into alliance, forget the fee for now. When we be again solvent, it will be time to settle our mutual accounts. Now excuse me; I must to my rest.''

* * *

Thorolf left Bardi's house well before dawn. Back at the Green Dragon, whose guests were not yet stirring, he found the room empty. Yvette had taken her beautiful new clothes and her reticule, including the contract offered to Thorolf, and vanished. Vasco had not seen her go.

Thorolf hastened back to Bardi's house, finding the iatromage at his meager breakfast. The soldier reported Yvette's disappearance.

"Curse of the green slime!" cried Thorolf. "I should have locked her in, or tied her to the bed, or something to restrain her. Now she'll have returned to the castle."

Bardi raised bushy gray eyebrows. "It would have accomplished nought. If I know aught of delta possession, she'd have climbed out the window, or screamed for help and asked Master Vasco to release her."

"Then I should have stayed and taken my chances on being able to refuse that indenture."

"But had ye remained steadfast in your refusal, she would still have departed."

"I could have held her by force."

"Then she'd have cried for help and charged you with kidnapping."

"I should natheless have thought of *something*. I am nought but an idiot." He pounded his skull with his knuckles.

"Take it not so to heart, Thorolf. Ye did your best, which is all any of us can do. Here, share my feeble fare. 'Twill cheer you up."

"I doubt that, Doctor," gloomed Thorolf. "But thanks anyway."

Fortified with Bardi's breakfast, Thorolf repaired to the barracks to take up his duties. After the morning's drill, he hied himself up Castle Hill. Over the castle gate, above the portcullis, workmen were installing a banner. This was a long yellow ribbon of yard-wide cloth

on which was painted in scarlet letters the legend:
SOPHONOMY SAVES THE WORLD!

Thorolf's heart beat faster, as it always did when he
thought he was nearing Yvette. As the gate guards
crossed their halberds before him, he said: "Pray in-
form Yvette, Countess of Grintz, that Sergeant Thorolf
would speak with her."

The guard soon returned, not with Yvette but with
the stout, red-haired, red-robed man with whom he had
spoken on his second approach to the castle. This one,
eyeing Thorolf coldly, said in a voice like a steel blade
on a grindstone:

"What do ye here, sirrah?"

"I wish to speak to Countess Yvette."

"Forsooth? Know that she does not wish to speak
with you."

Thorolf felt a flush of anger rising; he fought to keep
himself under control. "If you will send her out, or
admit me to where she is, she can tell me so in person."

"That is unnecessary. I have told you all you need
know; now depart and cease to trouble us."

"Pox on you!" shouted Thorolf as his self-control
began to slip. "You've put her under some damnable
spell, for which you shall answer to me!"

"Ye have mine answer," snapped the red-haired man.
Turning to the guards, he said: "Call out the duty
squad!"

The guard blew a whistle, and more mailed men bustled through the gate, drawing swords as they came.
The two on guard lowered their halberds, pointing the
spearheads at Thorolf's chest.

By reflex, Thorolf whipped out his own sword. He
was enraged enough to take on the whole duty squad
singlehanded, though the rational part of his mind knew
that he would be hacked to pieces in a trice. As the
guards crowded toward him, he backed warily toward

the downward path. If he could get them where they could only come at him one at a time . . .

"What's all this?" said a mellow voice, as Orlandus appeared. "Call off our hounds, good Parthenius. My dear Sergeant Thorolf! So you are fain to renew your pursuit of the Lady Yvette? Even after you rejected our perfectly reasonable offer?"

"Not reasonable at all. You wish me to become spellbound like the Countess. I demand that you exorcise the spirit possessing her and release her, forthwith!"

Orlandus chuckled. "My dear fellow! We cannot undertake so drastic a change in our program on your mere say-so. I'll tell you. Come in to drink and dine, and we'll discuss these matters. I am sure we can reach an amicable arrangement."

Thorolf snorted. "Me, enter that nest of vipers so you can have your men seize me and work your magic? How stupid do I look?" He had forgotten that, just before, he had demanded admission to the castle. "Send out Yvette!"

He made a slight motion with his sword. At once the men of the duty squad crowded forward, blades bared.

Orlandus sighed. "What a pity, to waste such a fine body and keen brain! Do your duty, men, to the foes of our Order!"

The guardsmen rushed forward, mail jingling. Thorolf, the first flush of whose rage had subsided, knew that, unarmored, he had no more chance against these bravos than the proverbial snowball in the fires of Mount Vasaetno. He ran down the path, easily outdistancing them and bearing with fortitude their shouts and jeers.

Thorolf walked the Street of Clockmakers furious, not so much with the Sophonomists as with himself, for having lost his temper in a circumstance that called for guile. He seldom let himself go so far, but once or twice a year the pressures built up and his composure ruptured. He should, he told himself, have had better sense than to voice loud demands upon his antagonists when he had no means of enforcing those demands. Thus he had achieved nought but to make himself look foolish.

Perplexed, he wandered across the city to Bardi's house. When the old wizard had dismissed his last client, Thorolf spent an hour fruitlessly mulling over plans for storming the Sophonomist stronghold, rescuing Yvette, and ridding her of the spell whereby Orlandus controlled her.

"Tell me something, Doctor," he said. "Meseems that all of Orlandus' folk who wore those yellow robes spake in that toneless voice, as if it proceeded from some contrivance mechanical. Does that mean that they were commanded by deltas—or, I should say, commanded by Orlandus through his deltas?"

"Aye, so I believe."

"And when he speaks of transforming selected followers into 'diaphanes,' he means merely those he has brought under deltaic possession?"

Bardi scratched his straggly beard. "Now that ye frame the thought, methinks ye be right."

"But the guards at the castle behave not thus, but as common mercenaries do everywhere."

"Let me think. . . . Ah! Belike I have it. Orlandus requires fighting men, dextrous in their deathly trade, however stupid in other respects. A delta lacks the practice and training to make its host a skillful man of his hands. For the same reason, whilst it can compel its human host to speak the words Orlandus hath commanded, it cannot imitate the tones of natural speech closely enough to deceive one who knows what to listen for."

Thorolf mused: "I follow your reasoning, Doctor. Now let's suppose that Orlandus gain control of the Rhaetian government, as he seems on the way to doing. He could little by little convert our soldiers to diaphanes, drilling and exercising each wight so possessed until the delta become as skillful with arms as its soldier host had erstwhile been."

"An ominous possibility, Thorolf."

"Aye, with more to come. What befalls a delta when its host dies?"

"I suppose it return to its own plane."

"Well, methinks I know enough of the art of war to realize that, be he never so brave, skilled, and zealous, the time comes when a soldier thinks: All is lost. If I remain, I shall be slain along with my comrades, to no good purpose. Then he begins to look about for escape. Orlandus' diaphanes, howsomever, will march fearlessly to their deaths, which mean nought to the deltas controlling them. This gives the cultmonger an advantage over any foes. Why, I can envisage his conquest of all the neighboring kingdoms and republics, even of the Empire. He must be stopped before his power waxes further!"

"Aye," said Bardi. "Alas that I am too old and feeble to face him! Ye must find sturdier allies for the deed."

Thorolf mused: "Doctor, are all of Orlandus' servants, save his soldiery, thus enslaved?"

"Methinks not; only those in yellow. Those holding positions of puissance in his conspiracy remain normal; one tells them by their crimson robes. Those in gray, the largest group, are the probationers. He sucks them dry of their wealth and extorts from them menial labor gratis. When their money is gone for his alleged 'courses,' he imposes deltas upon them and calls them diaphanes. Right clever, eh?"

"Would it not imperil Orlandus if some of the red robes, being less surely under his control, conspired to oust him and seize all power and pelf for themselves?"

"True, my son," replied Bardi. "But that is ever the dilemma of the leader. As I have said, deltas are unintelligent and thus pose no threat to him who commands them. But no leader can minutely oversee every act of a multitude of followers, however abjectly obedient. Hence he must have able, intelligent subordinates to serve him; and able subordinates may conceive ambitions of their own."

"Who are Orlandus' officers?"

Bardi waved his hands helplessly. "Little is known of the inner workings of his empire, save that he hath a lieutenant, clept Parthenius."

"I have met Master Parthenius," growled Thorolf. "He is the sort to whom, if he were drowning, I should be happy to throw an anvil. Any others?"

"Likewise he hath a treasurer, hight Cadolant, whom I believe unpixilated. There are others, but I know them not.

"Now I shall run a divination anent that squad of Carinthians who take such an unwonted interest in a respectable sergeant of the Rhaetian Army."

Daylight was fading when Thorolf, his suspicion of the Duke of Landai's men confirmed by Bardi's divination, approached the barracks. A voice spoke out of the deepening dark:

"Hist! Thorolf!" It was Sergeant Regin, who had often chaffed Thorolf on his virginity.

"Aye?" replied Thorolf. "What is't?"

"Keep in the shadows and whisper," muttered Regin. "First, go not into the barracks!"

"Why not?"

"There's a plot against you. If ye show your face therein, 'twill be the ax or the rope."

"Good gods! What's all this?"

"During the day, a fellow in a yellow coat rode up, handed the sentry a packet, and departed. The packet was addressed to the Colonel, old Gunthram himself. By a few shrewd questions, I learnt that the packet encompassed treasonable correspondence betwixt you and the Court of Carinthia, setting forth plans for the conquest of Rhaetia."

Thorolf pressed his lips together. "And you believed it not?"

"Such treasons and stratagems from my innocent pure-in-heart? Nay; I know you too well."

"Methinks I could prove these letters forgeries. He of the yellow jacket sounds like one of Orlandus' minions."

"Chance it not, Thorolf! The officers' quarters buzzed like a nest of angry wasps. Gunthram never did take to your promotion, holding scholars too airy-fairy daydreamy to be trusted with military duties. He brought the officers' council around to his way of thinking."

"If you can call what he does thinking," muttered Thorolf.

"True; but it remains that, step inside yon gate and ye are a dead man. Here, I've collected some of your chattels, with some food." Regin handed over a backpack and a crossbow.

"You're sure of this?" said Thorolf hesitantly.

"Aye forsooth! Here's a broadside fresh from the press, which they've made up in case ye failed to report back."

Thorolf fumbled in the pack and brought out his igniter and tinderbox. Having charged the chamber with tinder, he cocked the device and pulled the trigger. A click preceded a shower of sparks, and the tinder blazed up. Thorolf held the crudely printed paper in the wavering yellow light and read: REWARD FOR CAPTURE, DEAD OR ALIVE, OF THOROLF ZIGRAMSON, FORMERLY ACTING SERGEANT OF . . .

The flame went out. Thorolf said: "Whither should I flee? North to Carinthia or south to Tyrrhenia?"

"Neither! They've already sent out men to guard the passes. After this yellow-coated rogue departed, a squad in the dress of traveling merchants inquired after you in the barracks. 'Twas thought they were Carinthians, which did convince the waverers amongst the officers that ye were indeed a traitor."

Thorolf grunted. "That's what in literature we call irony. Those are men of Duke Gondomar of Landai, seeking to slay me."

"What hath Gondomar against you?"

"I rescued a damsel from his clutch."

"What'll ye do? Hide in the city?"

"Nay; with Gondomar's men, and the Sophonomists, and mine own comrades looking for me with no kindly intent, my chances were those of a pollywog in a pond of pike. I'll hie me into the higher mountains."

"Ye'll get lost or fall off a cliff!"

"I know the land well; I've spent many leaves in climbing. Three years since, I went thither with Professor Reccared of the college and a troll guide, seeking beasts for the Zoölogical Park."

"The trolls will devour you!"

"Methinks I can handle trolls; I know several in the mountains. And what alternative is there? Didst include any of my money in this pack?"

"Nay; to withdraw it from the regimental bank were sure to arouse suspicion." Regin hauled out his purse. "I can let you have a few pence. 'Tis all I have; I lost the rest gaming with File Leader Munderic. But what about your mare? She'll not be easy to take from the stables by stealth."

"I'm leaving her in your care," said Thorolf. "Whither I'm going, a horse were more hindrance than help. Thanks for the money. When I return, I'll repay you the principal in cash, with interest in the form of tales of mine adventures. Good night!"

Thorolf walked swiftly back to Doctor Bardi's house. If the old wizard did not use the wrong formula and turn him into an olifant, Bardi could put a temporary spell of illusion on him. Thorolf might also, he hoped, be able to touch Bardi for a loan. A man on the dodge needed money, and some upland peasants were a tight-fisted lot.

At the iatromage's house, Thorolf was surprised to see the door ajar. Either Bardi was becoming more woolly minded than ever, or . . . Just in case there might have been intruders, Thorolf laid hand on hilt and pushed his way in.

All was dark. Thorolf moved as silently as a stalking cat. He felt his way down the hall to the sanctum, the door of which was ajar. Silence lay as thick as the lid of a coffin.

He fired his igniter. The yellow flame showed a room in disorder—even greater disorder than usual. A chest had been upset, dumping out its contents. Books had been pulled from the shelves and scattered. Thorolf's boot struck one of the skulls lying on the floor; the cranium rolled away half a turn, seeming to grin up at him.

Before his light went out, Thorolf spied an unlit candle in a copper candlestick atop a row of books. He recharged and fired the igniter and got the candle lit. By the yellow light he espied a human foot projecting from behind a settle. He moved quickly; the foot proved to be that of Doctor Bardi, who lay supine with his throat cut.

Thorolf grunted. While he and Bardi had never been close, he had known the old wizard for years, had applied to him for the cure of ailments, and had become fond of him despite the mage's failing powers. He wondered: Was it common robbers, or Gondomar's men, or the Sophonomists who had slain the mage?

He thought the last the likeliest. Orlandus had learned from Yvette that Thorolf had rejected her offer. Thorolf had heard that Sophonomists were implacable toward traitors and apostates. Their leader assured them that they might, without guilt or qualm, cheat, betray, assault, rob, or slay those hostile to the Cause.

Thorolf had shrugged off such remarks as the typical inflation of rumors; but the speaker had evidently known whereof he spoke. They might well have added the

name of Thorolf Zigramson to their list of enemies.
Perhaps they thought that Bardi had advised him to reject Yvette. . . .

He scrutinized the room. The murder must have occurred at least an hour earlier, soon after Thorolf had
left Bardi's house the last time. Bardi's blood, black in
the candlelight, was fast drying but was not yet altogether dry.

So there was no point in crying the haro. The killers
would have escaped; if Sophonomists, they would be
back in their castle. From what Chief Constable Lodar
had told him, there would be little use in setting the
Constabulary after them. In fact, if Thorolf were found
here, he would become the prime suspect. While he
avidly yearned to bring the killers to book and to avenge
his friend, it began to appear as if it would be all he
could do to assure his own continued existence.

The settle behind which lay the corpse had not been
overturned, but the seat lid had been raised and the
contents scattered. Bardi had kept his dirty clothing in
the settle, awaiting the weekly visits of the washerwoman. Beneath the soiled garments he also kept a
small chest containing a substantial sum in gold; this
chest was now missing. Thorolf had advised the wizard
to put the money in a bank; but Bardi, having once been
burned in a bank failure, was bank shy. He had assured
Thorolf that the chest was securely locked by a spell;
but Thorolf knew that such spells were easily cancelled
by any competent magician.

Thorolf wondered how to get out of Zurshnitt. The
army would surely have alerted the gate guards, and
Bardi had not lived to put an illusion spell upon him.
He still had the protection of Bardi's counterspell against
illusions and possession, but that would wear off erelong.

Thorolf hunted until he came to a wardrobe holding
Bardi's spare robes. He chose a loose one bedight with
magical symbols and pulled it on over the knapsack.

A half-hour later, limping heavily, bent to look hunchbacked, and leaning on Bardi's walking stick, he came to the West Gate. When challenged, he said in a disguised voice:

"I be Doctor B-Bardi's new apprentice, F-Fermin by n-name, may it p-please the gallant captain."

With a bored wave, the soldier signaled Thorolf to proceed. Thanking the small histrionic skills that he had obtained by taking part in amateur plays at the university at Genuvia, Thorolf vanished into the night.

VI
EMPYREAN EXILE

Along the higher valleys of the Sharmatts, Thorolf Zigramson plodded unhappily upward, ever upward. On either hand rose the somber green, conifer-clad slopes; above these the iron-gray screes; and beyond these the glaring white of snow and glaciers. With the great love of his life in the goëtic grip of Orlandus and three sets of enemies seeking his gore, his hopes of an academic career and of union with his beloved seemed farther off than ever.

He felt grossly inadequate. True, his officers had often praised him for bringing his men up to standard in equipment, discipline, and general conduct; they had dangled promises of promotion. But he uneasily felt that his soldierly success had been at best a lucky accident. Any time, some untoward event would expose him as an incompetent impostor.

He marched grimly on. At least, he had come through recent armed encounters unscathed. A professor at Ge-

97

nuvia, Doctor Vipsanio, preached the philosophy called Chaoticism, which Thorolf found consoling. The burthen was that life, nature, and the universe were so unpredictable, and man so at the mercy of unforeseeable events, that one should neither give up hope in a parlous strait nor think that any success had made one proof against future disasters.

Since Thorolf had no camping equipment, he had slept in barns whose owners furnished an overnight hayloft and a meal in exchange for stories and gossip. The third day out, he was getting into the heart of the Sharmatts, above the treeline. A few late-blooming flowers gleamed in the scanty meadows. The barns had ceased, and the snowline lay not far above.

Thorolf thought he could handle trolls, from his experience with Doctor Reccared's guide and with the few he had met on fishing trips into the Dorblentz Range. He rehearsed the expected meetings. Thus he was not startled when a troll stepped out from behind a boulder and pointed an iron-tipped spear, croaking in Trollish:

"Who ye?"

Thorolf had learned Trollish from his few contacts and some book study. Shifting Bardi's walking stick to his left hand to free his sword arm, he answered:

"Me friend."

"So?" said the troll, approaching with a broad grin on its wide mouth, displaying large yellow teeth. The creature was the height of a short human being but so massively muscular as to make Thorolf, as strong as any man in his company, feel puny. Beneath its beetling brows gleamed pale-blue, sunken eyes, a wide, flat nose, and a receding chin half concealed by a scanty beard of tawny-yellow hair like that which clothed its barrel-shaped torso and stubby, thewy limbs. Trolls wore no clothes, their fur providing adequate cover. This one said:

"No goat?"

"No goat? What mean?" said Thorolf, puzzled.

"Who you, lowlander weakling?" demanded the troll, ignoring Thorolf's question.

Thorolf identified himself, adding: "Me know Chief Yig, in Dorblentzes."

"Chief Yig? Ah!" The troll put a little bone whistle to its mouth and blew. A dozen other yellow-furred, blue-eyed trolls emerged from behind the rocks and leisurely strolled toward Thorolf, grinning. All bore spears, bows, or slings.

"Say know Yig," the first troll told its fellows.

"Ah!" said the other trolls in chorus, moving closer. "Yig you friend?" asked one.

"Aye; us blood brothers."

"Ah!" said the trolls together. With a lightning rush, they sprang upon Thorolf from every side. Before he could draw a weapon, they had seized his arms and legs in a grip of inhuman strength and threw him supine. If they had been human, he would have given a good account of himself; but he was like a doll in the trolls' hairy hands. Keeping his composure with effort, he said:

"What is? Me friend!"

"You Yig friend," said the first troll. "Yig us foe. So you us foe."

It occurred to Thorolf that he should have looked into the shifting feuds and alliances among the trollish tribes before he ventured into their lands. He said:

"Me no harm. What you do?"

"You see," said the first troll. Four trolls, one gripping each limb, picked Thorolf up and bore him along the trail. To his demands, they merely grinned and replied:

"You see!"

After an hour in this painful position, Thorolf was borne into a kind of natural amphitheater, around which the mouths of several caves gaped in the hillside. The area was dotted with tents of hide and swarmed with trolls of both sexes and all ages. The air was thick with rough trollish voices, the clang of a forge, and an overpowering stench of unwashed bodies and rotting garbage.

At the farther end of the depression, a smelting oven rose against the hillside, sending up a plume of orange flame against the darkling sky. Trolls bustled about it. Others emerged from the nearest cavern mouth with sacks on their bent backs, which they emptied on the piles of minerals surrounding the smelter. Nearby, a troll was forking browse into a pen containing a dozen goats.

Trolls clustered about the arriving party, croaking questions. The trolls bearing Thorolf shouted: "Make way! Make way! Have meat!"

They approached a formidable-looking troll with a necklace of bear claws, who sat on a boulder whittling arrow shafts. Deftly removing Thorolf's sword and dagger, the captors set him on his feet, while two retained their grip on his arms.

"Who ye?" said the large troll.

Thorolf repeated his identification and added: "Who you?"

The big troll chuckled and replied in fluent if heavily accented Rhaetian: "My good fellow, ye have the honor of addressing Chief Wok, ruler of the Sharmatt trolls. Since ye have trespassed without leave on our lands, without bringing tribute, and since the dragon hath taken many of our goats, we find that we must needs use you to balance our diet."

"Dost mean to eat me?" cried Thorolf.

"Aye," said the troll.

Doctor Reccared, Thorolf remembered, had a theory that tales of trollish man-eating were merely a reflection of racial prejudice, and that they never ate human beings. Reccared, he thought, should be in his boots right now. He said:

"If you do this, it will cause you endless trouble with

the Zurshnitters. I am a respected sergeant in the Rhaetian Army.''

Wok merely chuckled again.

Thorolf raised his voice: ''They'll send an army and slaughter your folk, the innocent with the guilty!''

Wok wagged a thick forefinger. ''My dear fellow, we shall make sure that nought of you or yours remain in such form that the deed could be traced to us. Your garments, however necessary to lowland weaklings, are of no use to us; they shall therefore be burned. We shall make new hilts for your weapons, to fit our larger hands.''

''How do you plan to cook me?'' asked Thorolf.

The troll chief pointed to the center of the clearing. A large iron pot was suspended by a gantry over a fire laid but not lit. ''We shall boil you, of course,'' said Wok.

Thorolf fought to retain his composure. ''Not alive, I hope!'' he said in a casual tone, as if that were merely a minor inconvenience.

''Nay, nay. It were too much of a struggle to get you into the pot alive. Ye shall be well dismembered.''

''I knew not that you trolls could make so big a cauldron,'' said Thorolf. As he spoke, he frantically searched his memory for something he had heard or read.

Wok chuckled. ''That is our smith's masterpiece. It took endless hammering and reheating and filing to make it watertight.''

''Tell me, O Chief, how come you to speak such excellent Rhaetian?''

''Why not? Am I not a graduate of your Horgus College?''

''Indeed? That's unusual!''

''I'll tell you, since ye should have a tale to lighten your final hours. Years ago, ere ye were born, some well-meaning lowlanders thought, if trolls possessed the fruits of lowland education, they would turn into fellow lowlanders. So the then chief, my uncle Tep, chose five likely lads, including me, and sent them to Horgus.

"I boast not when I say that, of the five, I was the only one to do well with the language; the others could speak it only brokenly. When we completed our courses, five years later, we returned to the Sharmatts, as ye lowlanders call them. That is, all returned save poor Zid, who perished of some lowland disease.

"I fear we disappointed Chief Tep. We had picked up a smattering of Rhaetian; we had learned that the world was round; we could eat as ye do, with knives and those new Tyrrhenian things called forks. We had also acquired a taste for strong drink and insisted on wearing those woven things ye lowlanders cover your bodies with. Amongst us they are not only useless but also harbor vermin.

"Worse yet, we had lost all our trollish skills. We could not milk a she-goat, or guard the flocks against wolves and bears, or track ibex and chamois, or scale a cliff, or make fire by rubbing sticks. We could not endure to be out in foul weather. In other words, we were good for nought.

"One by one, my comrades perished. Yub fell off a cliff. Mro was fool enough to attack a dragon single-handed and was devoured. Nak went back to Zurshnitt and was last seen begging in the streets for money to buy your crazy-water.

"Seeing the results of lowland learning, I devoted myself to proper trollish skills and did not badly. When Uncle Tep died, the tribe, reasoning that I could better deal with the lowland menace because I spake lowlandish, chose me as chief.

"A few years past, some Zurshnitters came up to make us a similar offer, to train some of our youths. I declined but proposed in turn to train a number of their youths in our skills and make real men of them!"

"Very wise," said Thorolf. "What's this about tribute?"

"If ye would enter our lands," said Wok, "ye must first get my leave. When ye arrive, ye must bring this tribute, which we set at two goats per lowlander." Wok pointed to the pen with the goats. "See yonder? That is the tribute brought earlier today by a party of mountain climbers from Madjino, where they speak Tyrrhenian. Why lowlanders should come up here to climb for pleasure, I cannot fathom; but they do. They hope to ascend Mount Viggos ere the snows of winter forbid."

Thorolf said: "With due respect, has no one told you that it is wrong to eat your own kind?"

Again Wok uttered that irritating snicker. "Aye; four summers past, a preacher of one of your lowland cults came, calling upon us to accept his true faith. Since we found him amusing, we let him live a while.

"Then another preacher came, from the West, and another from the East. These three fell to quarreling, one claiming there was but one god; another, that there were two; and the third that there were three. In time we wearied of their screaming. They were delicious, especially the monotheist." Reminiscently, Wok picked his teeth with a splinter from the arrow shaft he was shaving.

Thorolf felt sweat beading his brow. "Would you not say it were right to do as one is done by?"

"I suppose so," said the chieftain.

"Well then, we Zurshnitters do not eat trolls. So by what right do you eat us?"

"Ye lowlanders may not eat of our flesh, but ye have natheless eaten our country."

"How mean you?"

"Ye stole our land!" roared Wok with clenched fists. "Once we roamed the entire ranges of the Helvetians and many lands besides. Then ye spindly, hairless creatures came. Having better weapons, ye drave us into the mountains. Ye fetched new diseases, whereof myriads of us perished. Year by year ye forced us higher into the ranges. When we protest, ye offer a new treaty, which ye no sooner sign than ye begin to violate. Now ye have devoured all the apple save the core, and some have designs on that as well.

"Ye tell us one should not eat one's own kind; but whose kind are we? I know your Senator Zigram proposed to recognize us as fellow beings. With mine own ears I heard your Senate howl the proposal down as the greatest jest in years."

Thorolf frowned. "With your own ears? You cannot have been in the Senate chamber. Hast magical powers?"

Wok winked. "Ah! Ask me no questions and ye shall hear no taradiddles. By the way, is that Senator Zigram the same as he who now sits as consul?"

"Aye; he is. He is also my father."

"Ah!" said Wok. "Every lowlander who wishes something of us doth claim he be a brother or son or cousin of some great lowland chief, thinking to overawe us. We have swallowed that bait too often to believe such a tale anew.

"But hold! Edifying though this talk be, we cannot continue it for ay. Your coming relieves us of the need to slaughter goats." To the trolls holding Thorolf, Wok said: "Take, cut up, boil!"

Thorolf struggled, shouting: "But he really is my father!"

The trolls nevertheless hauled him toward a large wooden block, behind which stood a troll with an oversized cleaver.

"Chief Wok!" Thorolf shouted, seeking an idea to forestall his demise. "It is proven impossible for so advanced a folk to practice cannibalism!"

"Eh?" said Wok. "Ye, a lowlander, presume to say what is impossible to *me*?" To the trolls he added: "Bring back!"

"Aye, sir!" said Thorolf. "A professor at Genuvia University explained it. When a folk has advanced so far in handicraft as to make cauldrons, they will have given up cannibalism. So the old jests about cannibals boiling outsiders in stewpots mean nought. It were what they call an anachronism, like Rhaetians fighting with stone axes."

"Hm," said Wok. "That shows how much your learned professors know. We may be advanced enough to make cauldrons but not enough for ye lowlanders to accord us the rights ye do each other."

Thorolf had an inspiration. "Chief, you said a dragon is taking your goats."

"That is so."

"A male or a female dragon?"

"A female."

"Why haven't your brave tribesmen slain the beast?"

"By day it lurks in its cavern, where it is certain death to venture. It issues forth at night to raid our herds by stealth. Several who have attacked it in the dark have perished."

"Could I but rid you of this dragon, were that not a fair price for my life?"

Wok snorted, his broad mouth turning down in an expression of contempt. "If our brave warriors have failed, think ye a lowland weakling would fare better?" In Trollish: "Take back to block."

"Wait!" shouted Thorolf. "You prize gold, do you not?"

"Aye, since we learned that this pretty but useless metal can be traded for lowland things and used to bribe lowland officials to leave us alone."

"Could I get rid of the dragon and also get you a lusty sum in gold, how would that be?"

"How much?" demanded Wok.

"Let us say a thousand marks."

"Not enough." In Trollish: "Take back!"

As he was dragged toward the block, Thorolf kept raising his bid. But Wok was obdurate, even when Thorolf had reached his ceiling of ten thousand. When the trolls had forced Thorolf to his knees and one had pulled

his head by the hair across the block, and the butcher-
executioner had raised his cleaver, Wok said:

"This time, methinks, ye speak sooth." In Trollish:
"Let go!" To Thorolf again: "How mean ye to slay
this beast? Hast a magical sword?"

It occurred to Thorolf that if he had stopped at a
lower ceiling, say five thousand, Wok would probably
have accepted that offer. But it was too late for that now.
He said:

"Nay; merely the common hanger your people took
from me. Against a beast so large and tenacious of life,
'twere no more effective than a flywhisk. I have another
scheme, for which I shall need a goodly length of
braided leathern rope, some sapling trunks, and the help
of your lustiest trolls."

"Ah! I do perceive ye plan some sort of snare. Ye
shall have your chance, albeit it grieves me to have the
goodly repast ye'd furnish end up in the dragon's belly
instead of in my people's. Blame me not if the beast
escape your trap and devour you!"

"In that case, I shan't be in condition to blame anyone. Meanwhile—"

"Aye, aye, ye shall have food and lodging until your
gin be ready. I trust your finical lowland gorge rise not
at roasted goat!"

"Thanks," said Thorolf. "One thing more. I relish
not the idea that, after I have overcome your dragon,
you will find some further pretext for devouring me."

"Sirrah! I brook no insults—"

Thorolf held up a hand. "Easy, good my chief. All
I ask is that each of us swear by that which he holds
most sacred—I by the antlers of our god Kernun, you
by the spirits of your ancestors."

Wok flinched. "How know ye that I cannot break
such an oath?"

"I study these matters," said Thorolf with feigned
nonchalance. He privately blessed Professor Reccared,

who in his lectures had included this bit of lore along with much misinformation about the trolls.

"Oh, very well," grumbled Wok. "Ye shall swear first."

Five days later, the rising sun was tinting the snows on the eastern flanks of the peaks a rosy pink, when a gaggle of golden-furred trolls, bearing ropes and poles and led by Thorolf, neared the dragon's cave. The mouth of the cave was a darksome blot on a rocky hillside. The scree that had spilled out included stones of all sizes, from pebbles to boulders.

Motioning the trolls to stand back and remain silent, Thorolf approached the cave mouth. He cocked an ear toward the darkness within and stood immobile, listening. At last he made out an intermittent sigh that was not quite a snore.

"Good!" he whispered. "Dragon sleep. Put poles here and here. . . ."

When places were found into which the poles could be thrust between the stones of the scree, Thorolf directed the rigging of his snare. Then he divided his score of trolls into two equal parties. Each group took the free end of a rope and retreated to one side of the cave, where they hid behind boulders.

Back at the cave mouth, Thorolf loaded one of the trolls' slings. He shouted: "Ho, dragon! Come forth!"

Receiving no reply, he whirled the sling and let fly. The slingstone struck a wall of the cave and rebounded, rattling. Thorolf repeated his challenge.

This time he heard a sleepy grunt. He fitted another stone and slung it; he was rewarded by a meaty thump. There was a loud, groaning roar, followed by a scrabbling of claws on stone.

"Come on, dragon!" yelled Thorolf. "Here I am!"

The scrabbling came closer; and presently a large, pearl-gray, reptilian head emerged from the cave, its golden eyes blinking in the sudden sunlight. The dragon had a long crocodilian muzzle and jaws full of curved ivory spikes. Its powerful scaly legs, furred with silvery bristles, raised its belly a good yard above the ground.

"Yah! Yah!" shouted Thorolf, capering. The monster shook its great head as if it could not believe its gemlike eyes. Then, roaring, it started for Thorolf at a shambling trot, yawning to show its scarlet gorge.

Thorolf scrambled down the rocky slope, guiding the dragon's course between the poles on either side of the cave. From the poles hung two large loops of rope. As the scaly head penetrated the loops, Thorolf shouted: "Pull!"

The trolls popped out of hiding, each grasping a section of rope. All backed away from the dragon, so that the two loops, falling from the poles, tightened around the reptile's neck.

The dragon checked its rush and swung its head right and left. When it lunged to its right at the trolls pulling on the rope on that side, the trolls on the other side braced themselves and pulled. The dragon then lunged to the left, with a similar result. It swiped at its neck with one of its forefeet, trying to get its claws beneath the strangling loops. Thorolf held his breath; if the beast severed either loop, he would call to the trolls to flee and take his own advice.

Just then six Rhaetians, clad for mountaineering in jackets of festive reds and greens and poling themselves along with hooked staves, hove in sight around one of the larger boulders at the bottom of the scree. They spied the dragon just as the dragon sighted them. With yells of terror, they ran back down the slope, casting away their staves.

At the sight of fresh meat fleeing, the dragon seemed to forget about the snare and the trolls. With a mighty roar, it started down the scree, jerking the trolls off their feet and weakening their grip on the rope. The dragon plunged after the fleeing mountaineers, dragging behind it the ropes and the few trolls who had retained their grip. These came down the slope in great leaps to keep up with their quarry. After them ran Thorolf and the remaining trolls. Thorolf shouted:

"Catch rope! Catch rope!"

This proved difficult, since on the slope the dragon moved as fast as man or troll. At length the whole procession was brought to a halt by a crag protruding from the lower slope. Thorolf shouted in Rhaetian and then in Tyrrhenian:

"Not that way! You'll be cornered!"

The climbers continued on until they fetched up at the bottom of a concave angle in the crag. Here they huddled helplessly as the dragon lumbered toward them.

Under Thorolf's shouted directions, the trolls whom the dragon had shaken off secured their grip on the rope once more and braced themselves to restrain the monster. He had, Thorolf realized, underestimated the dragon's strength; he should have employed at least twice as many trolls.

Closer came the dragon to the huddled Rhaetians, who screamed in terror. Thorolf thought, while he did not crave a hero's death, since he had started the episode he bore a responsibility.

He sprang in front of the dragon with drawn sword. "Get back!" he shouted and whacked the dragon's muzzle with the flat of his blade.

The dragon blinked, jerked back, and gave another roar. As again it extended its fangsome head, Thorolf struck it again. When it tried to turn away to one side, he hit it on the side of its muzzle; when it turned the other way, he hit it on the other side.

It seemed to Thorolf that he had been whacking the scaly muzzle for hours, although the time was less than a quarter-hour. Then the dragon, evidently suffering a sore nose, tried to back away. Dragging screeching trolls after it, it laboriously turned, tangling the ropes, and began to plod back up the slope.

As it forged on toward the mouth of its cave, it slowed

like an unwound Rhaetian clock. Halfway to its goal it collapsed on the stones, breathing in gasps. The chase, thought Thorolf, must have winded it, and to drag a score of trolls back up the hill with its windpipe half strangled by the two nooses was too much for its reptilian constitution.

"Tie mouth!" cried Thorolf. Soon the dragon's jaws were bound together by several turns of spare rope around its muzzle.

"Now legs!"

In another half-hour the dragon had been rolled over on its back and its limbs bound to its body. It protested by feeble writhings. The troll whom Thorolf had appointed foreman of his crew said:

"Now kill?"

"No kill. Take Zurshnitt, sell."

The troll snorted. "Lowlanders crazy!" A gabble broke out among the trolls as they digested Thorolf's intentions.

Thorolf said: "More rope, more poles. Make sled."

As the trolls scattered to obey, the Rhaetians approached Thorolf. Their leader, in an orange jerkin, said: "A troll doth tell me ye roused this beast from its lair and sent it charging after us! This is an outrage!"

"I was merely capturing the dragon," said Thorolf, "when you came along. If you had watched where you were going . . ."

His words were drowned out by a chorus of protest: "Endangering peaceful citizens!" "Reckless folly!" "Gross negligence!" "Ye shall hear from mine attorney!"

When, shouting, they pressed close to Thorolf, he roared back: "I faced the creature at my own risk to protect you lubbers! Now get you hence, or . . ."

He drew his sword. At the sight of the blade, the unarmed Rhaetians straggled off, muttering threats of litigation.

* * *

The setting sun was painting the western slopes of the peaks with streaks of crimson when the trolls conveyed the trammeled, silver-gray dragon to their campsite. Beginning to recover from its earlier exertions, the beast protested by writhing and grunting through its nostrils. Chief Wok appeared, saying:

"By my grandsire's ghost, what is this? I thought ye might come back with the hide and flesh, but not a live, wriggling monster! Think ye to make a pet of it? I warn you, 'twill never become a safe housemate!"

"That's your ten thousand marks," said Thorolf. "Know you Doctor Berthar, who directs the Zoölogical Park in Zurshnitt?"

"Aye, he was here some years agone, seeking a rare butterfly, which meseems a strange thing for a grown man, even a crazy lowlander, to do. I mislike dealing with those gentry, because they once shut some of us in cages with their beasts. That was an insult!"

"Like it or not," said Thorolf, "he has the money wherewith to buy one healthy female dragon, hoping to mate her with their male. All you need do is to send a brace of trusty trolls to Zurshnitt with a message. Let Berthar send out a gang of workmen with a wagon, to meet your trolls with the dragon halfway and hand over the money."

"I like this not," growled Wok. "If I know you low-landers, the instant my people cross into the lands the Zurshnitters stole from us, they are liable to a bolt in the brisket. I alone speak enough Rhaetian to deal with these folk, but I must needs remain here. Ye could accompany the dragon—but nay, nought would hinder you from escaping our grasp, taking the money with you."

"I'll write to Berthar," said Thorolf, digging into his scrip. He brought out a pad of paper, a battered quill, and a stoppered ink bottle.

"I still like it not, but money is money." Wok gave Thorolf a sinister smile. "Our agreement was that ye should slay the beast, not take it alive. The dragon's flesh would have fed the tribe for many days. Since that be not now in prospect, why should we not eat you?''

"Your pardon, O Chief," said Thorolf, "but if you recall the exact terms, I promised to 'get rid of' the dragon. Nought was said of how, whether by slaying or capture or merely driving it away from your lands. Besides, I could scarcely write to Doctor Berthar if I were dismembered and cooking, now could I?''

Wok grumbled: "Slippery, scheming lowlander! Very well, write your letter. But ye shall remain with us until the money be delivered.''

Thorolf, pen in hand, paused. "Since, O Chief, you have cast doubt upon mine own prospects, in return for the letter I ask that we enter into another pair of oaths, that I shall not be slain whatever betide. As for remaining here, I hope to do so for some little time. I will do my share of tribal labors.''

"Eh?" said Wok. "What lets you from returning to Zurshnitt?''

"Certain enemies have made that city unhealthy for me.''

"Ah!" said Wok. "Ye are a wanted man, then! Had I known sooner, I might have sold you back to those foes whereof ye speak.''

"You would not have obtained any ten thousand marks for my carcass. And now for the oaths. . . .''

VII
Nugacious
Nuptials

For the next fortnight, Thorolf Zigramson dwelt in the village of the Sharmatt trolls and took part in their simple toils and pleasures. Since he proved handy with tools, they set him the task of whittling arrow shafts and attaching feathers and iron heads. In his spare time he whetted his weapons, practiced shooting his crossbow and throwing his dagger, and washed his dirty linens and hose in the creek that served the settlement.

The trolls who had been sent with the captive dragon returned. Two bore a stout pole between them. From the pole hung a leathern sack, the weight of which made the pole sag. Evening found Chief Wok and Thorolf squatting by a fire and painstakingly counting out ten-mark gold pieces. The Chief had drafted Thorolf to keep a tally with little sticks, each representing ten coins.

When the count was over and a hundred sticks reposed in little piles, Wok said: "I am still not certain. This time ye shall count coins whilst I pile the sticks."

Thorolf counted. Although he had taken pains to count accurately, he only tallied 998 coins.

"Try again," growled Wok, taking over the coins. This time there was one coin left over when a hundred sticks had been piled.

Wok gave an angry roar. "These cursed things must be bewitched!"

"Wilt try once more?" Thorolf asked.

"Oh, to the spirit world with the futtering things! It is close enough. Thorolf, since ye have fulfilled your agreement, it is but fair that we should enlarge you. Whither go ye next?"

"For the time being," said Thorolf, "I should be happy to remain with the tribe, provided I may move about at will."

"Good!" roared Wok, smiting Thorolf on the back with numbing force. "Meanst to stay for ay and perchance take a mate from amongst us?"

The thought of a troll wife appalled Thorolf. He had gotten used to trolls but still found the females monstrously ugly. Still, in his present strait he dared not say so. Tactfully he replied:

"That were a great honor, Chief Wok. But I should have to think about it, since I already have mine eye upon a lowland female."

"Fetch her hither and mate with both!" said Wok. "Or better yet, keep one wife here and another in Zurshnitt. In such a case, it were better not to tell either of the other." He winked. "We'll talk of this anon. Meanwhile, hast ever hunted?"

"Aye, with my father."

Wok shot a sharp glance. "Who is your father?"

"I told you, Zigram Thorolfson, who as senator introduced that bill to make trolls human beings. As you know, he is now Consul of the Rhaetian Republic."

Wok's jaw dropped. "I disbelieved you when ye said

so before; but now we know you for a true man. Now that we truly know ye have this kinship, ye must assuredly mate with one of our tribeswomen, to bind you to us and give us influence with your government. I will find a nice girl. Meanwhile, ye should sharpen your skill at the hunt.'' Wok raised his voice to a bellow: ''Oh, Gak!''

Wok's eldest son strolled near. ''Aye, Father?''

Wok said: ''Thorolf true man; lowlander outside, troll inside. Take hunt tomorrow.'' The Chief turned back to Thorolf. ''This is worth getting drunk over. Gak, two beer!''

Soon Gak returned with two mugs of crude trollish pottery, filled with barley beer. Thorolf disliked the trollish beverage. The brew was not only weak but also so full of barley grains that it was best drunk through a straw. But there was no decent way to avoid it now.

Wok, less fastidious, drank his beer in great gulps, straining the grains out with his teeth and spitting them on the ground. Thorolf looked across the amphitheater to where several trolls were firing up the smelter. Other trolls ignited simple torches, made by dipping cattails in goat grease, before they disappeared into a nearby cave mouth. Thorolf felt the stirring of an idea. He asked:

''Oh Chief, whither goes the tunnel from yonder cave?''

''To bed of iron ore,'' said Wok with a hiccup. ''Wouldst like to see how we mine it?''

Thorolf suppressed a shudder, saying vaguely: ''Some day, mayhap.'' He did not wish to admit that he had an irrational fear of dark, narrow places, ever since as a boy he had been accidentally locked in a clothes chest. He went on:

''Is that all? Does a branch extend to Zurshnitt?''

''Nay, nay. What made you think of such a thing?'' Wok's gaze shifted furtively. Thorolf had been with trolls long enough to read their expressions.

L. SPRAGUE DE CAMP & CATHERINE CROOK DE CAMP

"We have legends," said Thorolf, "of trollish tunnels extending all over Rhaetia, even beneath the streets of our cities. Betimes politicians warn us that the trolls might burst out of their tunnels and massacre folk in their beds."

Wok finished his mug. "What stupid idea!" His Rhaetian deteriorated as the beer took effect. "Certes, we have tunnels, but not hence to Zurshnitt. Would be several days' walk, and who could bear enough food, water, and torches to last the distance? Besides, air bad."

"But you do have a tunnel under Zurshnitt?"

"Oh, yea; but ye enter it not here. Entrance less than hour from city—" Wok clapped a hand over his mouth. "Oh, sacred ancestors! I told you one of our deepest secrets. Too much beer. How knew ye of it?"

"You told me you had heard a session of the Senate, and I remembered the trollish tunnels."

"Lowlanders too damned clever. Is terrible sad."

"What is sad? I'll never tell—"

Wok began to weep. "Dare not let you go. Must eat you now." He dropped into Trollish. "You friend. Eat friend bad. No eat friend bad. No take chance."

"Be not a ninny!" cried Thorolf, disguising the fear he felt. "I'm practically a member of the tribe, so why should I harm you?"

Wok caught Thorolf's hand, a pleading expression on his brutish face. "You be real troll? Mate with troll girl? Good! Me get you nice girl. Oh, Gak!" he shouted.

"Aye, Father?" The young troll came on the run.

"You know Bza, Fid daughter?"

"Yea."

"Fetch. Her Thorolf mate."

The horrified Thorolf dared not protest for fear of the stewpot. The youth returned with a young female, even shorter and more barrel-shaped than most trollish women. Wok roared: "Bza, you good girl, fit Thorolf

116

mate. Him lowlander outside but troll inside. Him good man. You be good mate. Me say you, him mate. For night, me give own tent. Take, Thorolf. Have fun all night and many cubs!''

Wok rose to his feet, slapped Thorolf's back, lost his balance, and stretched his length on the turf. Gak bent over him, saying:

"You well, Father?"

The only response was a thunderous snore. Gak looked at Thorolf, whose gaze shifted from Wok to Gak to Bza. At last Gak said:

"Father lend tent. Come!"

Following Gak among the tents, Thorolf was startled when Bza caught his hand in her hairy one. He found the touch repellant, though Bza was only doing what was expected of her. At the big tent in the middle, Gak pulled aside the flap, thrust in his head, and cried:

"Out, Mother, aunts! Wedding!"

Several of Wok's wives emerged. One said to Thorolf: "You lowland weakling, take Bza mate? You be good mate, or all women of tribe beat shit out of you!"

"Have strong yard!" cried Gak, closing the tent flap behind Thorolf and Bza.

A little pottery lamp dimly lit the tent. A small iron pot in the center flickered and smoked; this took the edge off the autumnal chill but did not heat the tent enough to comfort a "lowland weakling." To one side lay a heap of bear and wolfskins.

Bza fingered Thorolf's jacket. "How can futter in false skin?" she asked.

"Come off," replied Thorolf, feeling more and more appalled. The sight and strong odor of Bza's squatty body aroused no lust whatever. What if he could not get it up? He had heard jokes about shepherds and ewes but had no such tendencies himself.

"Take off," said Bza. "False skin scratch." She lay down on the pile of skins and spread her stout, yellow-furred form.

In for a penny, in for a mark, thought Thorolf. One by one he shed his garments. At last he approached the supine troll girl with lagging steps, as if on his way to the headsman's block. This was certainly not the initiation into the pleasures of love about which he had fantasized. He began to shiver.

Bza raised herself on one elbow. "What matter? No stiff?" she said, pointing.

"Well—ah—" Perhaps if he shut his eyes and imagined Yvette. . . . Then Thorolf was startled to see, in the dimness, a tear trickle down Bza's hairy cheek; then another.

"Why, Bza!" he said. "You weep!"

Her wide mouth puckered, and she sobbed. "Sorry. Do duty. Come on, futter! Get over!"

"What matter? No want?"

"N-nay. Me try, but you so ugly! No hair on long, thin body, like snake!"

"No want, no do," said Thorolf, sneezing and sitting down beside her. He stroked her scalp as if she had been a pet animal. "No fear. Me kind." He sneezed again.

She sobbed more than ever, stammering: "M-me love. Love Khop. Few day, me Khop mate. Then you come."

"Be Khop mate," he said.

"No can. Wok say us mate."

"No worry. Me no say; you no say. No tell Wok. Me love other, too. Many days, me go; you be Khop mate. Good?"

"Good!" Bza threw her thick arms around Thorolf and gave him a hug that, he thought, came close to cracking a rib. He said: "Now sleep!" and blew out the lamp.

On the next day's hunt with Gak, Thorolf had to endure Gak's coarse jokes and unabashed curiosity about Thorolf's nuptials. He passed off Gak's remarks with vague nothings, and the young troll ceased after Thorolf, with a lucky crossbow bolt, brought down an ibex.

A few days later, returning from a similar hunt without game, Thorolf approached the little tent that Wok had assigned him. He was about to throw open the flap when a faint sound from within made him pause. The sound, he perceived, was that of heavy breathing from two occupants.

He wormed a finger into the crack of the flap, teased it open a hairsbreadth, and put his eye to the slit. Inside was still dark, but the thread of light through the crack glanced from the golden fur on the hindquarters of a male troll, rhythmically rising and falling. He could not see the other occupant but inferred that Bza was entertaining her disappointed suitor Khop.

Thorolf stealthily withdrew and sat down at a distance, facing so that he could watch the tent out of the corner of his eye as he worked on arrow shafts. It was nothing to him if the mate whom Wok had foisted on him took her former betrothed as lover; in fact he rather approved. It would dissuade her, he thought, from developing an amorous passion for her nominal mate. For all that she avowed him hideous, long propinquity could stimulate lust between the most unlikely pair.

A movement at the edge of his vision caught his eyes. A huge, burly young male troll emerged from the tent, glanced around with comical furtiveness, and slunk away. Thorolf pretended not to see him. Knowing the enormous strength of trolls, Thorolf thanked his paganist gods that he had not interrupted the tryst.

Another disquieting thought crossed Thorolf's mind. Suppose Bza conceived during these trysts? Would Thorolf be deemed the father and held responsible? He was hazy on trollish customs; but Rhaetia had stern laws on parental responsibility. Desertion of one's family, for instance, was punished by fifty lashes for the first offense, a hundred for the second, and so on upward until the offender expired.

It was high time that he attacked his problems in Zurshnitt. Any hue and cry over Bardi's murder should by now have died down. Besides, although inured to the hardships of life in a tent, Thorolf was getting tired of goat's meat, barley porridge, and weak beer.

After the evening meal, Thorolf sought out Wok, saying: "Chief, know you aught of the Sophonomists and their leader, the wizard Orlandus?"

Wok swelled his furry chest and smote it with his fist. "Vile catiffs! I hate them! If I had Orlandus here, I would twist his head off, slowly, and boil it for soup!"

"Why so?"

"He tells the stupid lowlanders we be evil beings, demons. When he hath power, he says he will kill us all—even the little ones because, he says, 'nits make lice'!"

"Hast heard him say this with your own ears?"

"Aye."

"So your tunnel under Zurshnitt has a branch beneath the old Castle Zurshnitt?"

"How knew ye?" barked Wok.

"Simple reasoning. Now harken, O Chief. I and my father and many other Zurshnitters also hate and fear these Sophonomists. But they are clever and dangerous. They put converts into posts in our government, where they steal documents. When people oppose Orlandus, he frightens them into silence, or casts a spell upon them, or bribes them, or harasses them with lawsuits, or—"

"What is a lawsuit?"

Thorolf explained. Wok picked up a club, the head of which was a ball set with iron spikes. "If any lowlander tried that on me, I would see if his head was harder than this!"

"Such a program would not work amongst lowlanders, any more than their laws and courts would succeed amongst trolls. Besides, Orlandus has servants possessed by spirits called deltas, which obey him without question.''

''What canst do?''

''I have a plan, and I need your help. First I must get in touch with my father, the Consul.''

''How?''

''I shall write a letter. The next time you send a party to your border to trade with the Zurshnitters, they can give this letter to one of the merchants.''

''Will this merchant pass it on to the Consul? Canst trust him?''

Thorolf shrugged. ''My father will pay the messenger for the service; and one must betimes take a chance. Then he and I shall confer, alone at a place I know. He will have bodyguards, but I shall tell him to keep them away.''

''Ah! Then I had better send trolls to guard you likewise,'' said Wok.

Thorolf shook his head. ''I fear not my father's men, since he and I are on good terms. Nobody else need know.''

Thorolf's letter read: THOROLF TO CONSUL ZIGRAM, GREETINGS. WILT MEET ME AT THAT POOL ON THE RISSEL WHERE YOU TAUGHT ME TO FISH? WE HAVE MUCH TO DISCUSS. SET DATE AND KEEP YOUR ESCORT OUT OF SIGHT AND HEARING.

On a drizzling day in autumn, Thorolf set out for the pool at which he had first met Yvette of Grintz. Because the peasantry might have heard he was wanted and seize him, he carried, folded up in his pack, a little one-man tent of hides. Under this he spent a damp, uncomfortable night.

During the afternoon of the second day he came to the Rissel. The fog made black ghosts of the trunks of the leafless trees and the wan fronds of the conifers. Away from the stream, the dominant sound was the constant drip of water.

Thorolf followed the river upstream to a rapid, where he could cross by leaping from boulder to boulder. Then he followed the riverbank down to the pool where he had been fishing when Yvette had manifested herself. As he came in sight of the misty flat, he saw a bulky figure, in official crimson, sitting on a folding stool and fishing. He speeded his approach, calling: "Father!"

The Consul heaved himself to his feet and embraced his son. "Well, Thorolf!" he said. "Thou lookst well."

"The simple mountain life, sir."

"But I fear thou also stinkest."

"Sorry about that; but where I've been there's no water deep enough to bathe in."

"Anyway, it joys me to see you alive and hale. Where hast been?"

"Living with the Sharmatt trolls. Is there a warrant out for my arrest?"

Zigram sank back on his stool, the feet of which settled into the watery soil beneath his weight. "Merely a summons as witness. Gunthram was hot to charge you with murder, desertion, and a treasonous plot with the Carinthians. I squelched that last accusation, pointing out that it came from the Sophonomists and should hence be handled with tongs; also that a band of rogues from Carinthia had attacked you in the Zoölogical Park—something to do with the fugitive Countess of Grintz."

"How about the murder? You know I'd never have harmed dear old Bardi."

"Lodar tells me they have taken in another suspect. The details I know not yet. As for desertion, I told Gunthram ye were on a secret mission for me."

Thorolf squatted, as living with trolls had accustomed him to do. "Where is Yvette now?"

The Consul shrugged. "As far as I know, your lady love is mewed up in the castle. None hath seen her since your departure. Now tell me the tale of your in-

volvement with that lady. I have never had it straight—
merely a hundred rumors, each contradicting the last.''

"Very well, Father. See you this place? 'Tis where
she and I first met. . . .''

Thorolf went through the story of his encounter with
the unclad Countess, Bardi's magical blunder, and her
subsequent capture by Psychomagus Orlandus.

"He has cast upon many followers," said Thorolf,
"a spell that causes them to be possessed by a spirit,
which enables him to command their implicit obedi-
ence. If he bade them jump off a cliff, they would do
it.''

"Terrible!" muttered Zigram. "I wish someone
would magic this accursed cult out of existence! As
things now stand, I can do nought, for reasons ye
know.''

"If I rooted out this nest of vipers, wouldst give me
all the protection your position commands?''

"Assuredly so! But ye must needs do a thorough job.
If ye let Orlandus and a few of's creatures escape, they'd
be back to plague us more. How would ye gain access
to his lair, defended by stout fortifications, fanatical followers, and magical spells?''

"Methinks I have a way," said Thorolf.

"How? Through those mythical trollish tunnels?''

Thorolf winced, feeling the testicular cringe that the
thought of entering a tunnel gave him. "I'll tell you
nought that they could twist out of you. Speaking of my
friends the trolls, knowst Orlandus' plans for them?''

"Aye. And I am he who tried to raise them to human
rank! But the cultists have me in a cleft stick—''

A loud sneeze made both speakers start. Each looked
at the other, saying, "Health!" before they realized that
neither had in fact sneezed.

Thorolf sprang up and raked the landscape with a
glance. Then he started away from the stream, saying:
"Father, come see!''

Thorolf was watching, at his own eye-level, a pair of

123

detached eyeballs hanging in midair. He could see the little red blood vessels forming a network around the interior of the eyeballs. As he watched, the eyeballs swiveled away and began to move off.

"Ho! Come back!" shouted Thorolf, reaching for his sword.

When the eyeballs continued to retreat, Thorolf bounded after them and swung his blade in a whistling arc. The sword met meat, and its unseen target pulled it down to the ground. Blood sprayed from an invisible source.

As Thorolf wrenched his blade loose, a faint, transparent human form, like a man-shaped fog, came slowly into sight. As it solidified, it became a man of medium stature and build, nude and clean-shaven, with a deadly wound where Thorolf's sword had cloven it between neck and shoulder, shearing down into lungs. The wound still bled, but the body showed no signs of life.

"Good gods!" Zigram exclaimed. "What's this, son? Hath some wizard made himself invisible to spy upon us?"

"I have a suspicion, Father. Bide you here whilst I seek evidence."

Thorolf soon returned bearing a pair of boots, breeches, and a yellow robe. He said: "Methought the knave would have hidden his garments nearby. Had he been invisible but his raiment not, we were as startled by an empty suit of clothes walking about as by the whole man. He was one of Orlandus' diaphanes, as the villain calls his pixilated victims."

The Consul said: "Doubtless he sent the fellow to follow me from the city. But why did the Psychomage not make the rascal's eyeballs invisible along with the rest of him? They enabled you to perceive and slay the fellow."

"My professor at Genuvia explained it. Sight comes from the mutual action of light rays and the eye. Were the eyeballs as transparent as the rest of him, the light would pass through unhindered, and the rogue were blind until the spell wore off." Thorolf held up the garments he had found. "Here's your evidence for legal action against the Sophonomists."

Zigram frowned. "I know not, son. If I bring action, Orlandus will claim this fellow acted on his own; and since the rascal's dead, that were hard to disprove. Besides, Orlandus hath the shrewdest attorney in Zurshnitt, Doctor Adolfo, in his pay. Moreover, ye know what they'd do to my repute—"

"Oh, you mean that damned election!" snorted Thorolf. "Where's your courage, man? Which—"

"Stand!" came a new command. From downstream a group of men marched forward, swords in hand. They wore merchants' dress of plain browns and blacks, but bits of mail gleamed dully underneath.

"Who are ye?" barked the Consul, drawing his own blade. Beside him, Thorolf whispered:

"Try not to provoke a battle, Father. You're too old for swordplay."

"And who impugned my courage just now?" rumbled Zigram. "I shall do what I must." Raising his voice, he called: "Wilchar! Odo! To me!"

The Consul's bodyguards came crashing through the bushes, armed, armored, and nocking arrows to bows. Zigram turned back to the newcomers. "Know that I am the Consul General of the Commonwealth of Rhaetia. Who are ye and what do ye here?"

"Let your Excellency not trouble himself," said the leader in the vernacular of Carinthia. "We seek two persons, to wit: Countess Yvette of Grintz and a knave who slew three of our comrades. That hulking man beside you fits the description. Who are ye, sirrah?"

"Concern yourselves not with that," said Thorolf. "You are Duke Gondomar's men, using our sovereign Commonwealth as your private hunting preserve."

"None of your affair—" began the leader, but Thorolf interrupted:

"As for the Countess, she's where neither you nor I have access to her."

"Meaning she's dead?" cried the Carinthian.

"She might as well be, being in thrall to a magician. Now get back to your Duke and cease to pester us." Thorolf turned to the bodyguards. "If it come to blows, how many can you kill ere they close with us?"

"At this range," said Odo, "two surely and four probably. They are seven, and methinks we four could account for the rest."

"So find your horses and gallop for the border," said Thorolf, "counting yourselves lucky to get out unscathed—"

"Hold!" said a new and toneless voice. A group of yellow-robed men approached from upstream with bared swords. The leader, who had spoken, continued in his flat, unmodulated tone: "We see ye have slain one of our number." He indicated the dead man. "Ye are all our prisoners. Resist not, or it will be the worse for you. Yield, and ye shall not be hurt."

Over a dozen yellow robes advanced, spreading out as if to surround both the Consul's men and the Carinthians.

Thorolf said to the Carinthian leader: "These are creatures of the sorcerer Orlandus. If they take us, he'll possess us, like them, with spirits that force us to obey his whims. We must join to fight them!"

"Shoot the yellows!" the Consul roared to his bodyguards.

Instantly two bows twanged. At that range, the arrows struck the chests of two Sophonomists with such force as to sink up to the feathering and protrude from their backs.

Although staggered, the two struck recovered and came on as if nothing had happened. Zigram's bodyguards got off two more arrows, with the same result. The Carinthian leader shouted to his men:

"They're walking corpses! Kill them!"

He sprang forward and struck a terrific backhand at the leading Sophonomist. The man's head flew off, struck the ground, and rolled. Spouting blood, the headless body continued forward, blindly slashing empty air.

"They cannot be slain!" wailed a Carinthian. "All's lost! Flee! Flee!"

As one, the party from Landai turned and ran, as fast as the weight of their mail allowed. They hastened downstream with a jingle and clatter of accouterments.

"Keep shooting!" shouted the Consul. The headless body finally sank to the sward.

Bows twanged, then swords were out and clanging. Thorolf's party formed a back-to-back group as the Sophonomists silently closed with them. Thorolf found them slow, clumsy fighters. He thrust one through and then, finding the fellow still in action, hewed his arm from his shoulder.

The man whose arm Thorolf had severed stopped to recover his sword with his remaining arm. Thorolf split his skull, whereupon the cultist slumped at last while two others pushed forward and tried to step over the body to get at Thorolf. While swinging swords with one hand, each of them reached out with the other to clutch at Thorolf. He hewed off both clutching hands, one at the wrist and the other at the elbow. Thereupon the two attackers dropped their swords and thrust their remaining hands toward Thorolf.

"They're trying to take us alive!" Thorolf cried, hacking two-handed at his maimed antagonists with chopping woodcutter's strokes. No matter how fiercely he and his allies fought, he thought, they were doomed by weight of numbers. As he thrust another through, the attacker seized the sergeant's sword with his free hand, ignoring the deep wound the blade made in his hand. Another aimed a blow at Thorolf's head, splitting his hat but not his scalp.

Another sound broke upon Thorolf's ears. From nowhere a horde of yellow trolls erupted and charged, waving iron-headed spears, axes, and clubs. Yelling, they rushed upon the Sophonomists from behind. Of some they spattered the brains with mighty blows; others they hewed asunder or picked up and threw into the Rissel.

In a few minutes it was over. Zigram, Thorolf, Wilchar, and Odo stood panting and sweating amid a ring of bodies, most of them dismembered like beeves in a butcher shop. Blood spattered the garments of the survivors as if it had been thrown at them by bucketsful. Nor was all the blood that of the Sophonomists; Thorolf had taken a slit in his skin along the ribs; his father had a wounded arm. The mailed bodyguards had fared better, but Wilchar's cheek bled copiously from a cut.

Looking up from tying bandages, Thorolf said in Trollish: "Hail, Gak! How come here?"

"Wok say, lowlanders play trick. Kill Thorolf. Thorolf good troll in lowlander body. Go watch. If see trick, help Thorolf!"

"Good!" said Thorolf. "This Consul. Troll friend. My father."

Gak ducked his head, grinned, and slapped Zigram on the shoulder, sending him staggering. "Ah! Good. Help us; we help you."

"Now both mine arms are lamed," grumbled the Consul, moving the bruised member. "What saith the troll?"

Thorolf translated. Zigram said: "Tell him I will do my best to get my bill anent trolls through the Senate. I owe it to his folk."

When Thorolf translated, and the trolls roared approval, Zigram added with a smile: "Pray, no more friendly slaps! That last all but dislocated my shoulder."

"Now," said Thorolf, "surely you have all the evidence you need to command an attack on Castle Zurshnitt!"

"Think ye so? Gunthram's convinced that so many of our men are secret Sophonomists that when so commanded, they'd turn on their own officers instead. Think not but that we've considered the problem. Moreover, Orlandus could use your Yvette as a hostage.

"I'll tell you! Proceed with this secret plan of yours. If by the time the election be over, Orlandus' flag still flies high, I'll see what I can do."

As Zigram and his bodyguards painfully prepared to mount and amble off, Thorolf said: "Father, how shall we communicate? We need something more regular than an occasional trading party."

Zigram shrugged. "I know not, son."

"Let's say you develop a burning thirst for trollish beer and have arranged to receive a keg thereof each week. We can have our missives exchanged with each load."

"That horrible stuff!"

"You could give it to your cat when no witnesses be nigh."

"And poison the poor beast? Anyway, she'd have better sense than to drink it."

"Well, send me some more paper, pray. I am almost bereft!"

Thorolf waved to the departing Consul and folded the garments that the invisible Sophonomist had worn. At least, Orlandus had not been so prescient as to realize that a naked spy in this cool, wet weather was likely to betray his presence by sneezing. He gathered his bundle and turned back toward the village of the Sharmatt trolls.

VIII
Dubious
Deliverance

Looking at Wok across the fire as they gnawed goat's meat, Thorolf said: "O Chief, I shall need help to overthrow the Sophonomists."

Wok took his time. "Get your father to declare us people, and we will help. Otherwise, not."

"Ah—a fine idea, but I know not how to bring it about. . . ."

"That is my final word, Thorolf. Any such venture were perilous to us trolls. Why lust ye after this? Hast not a good life here?"

"It's not that you treat me badly. I told you I had an eye on a lowland woman in Zurshnitt. She is a prisoner of Orlandus."

"What's wrong with Bza? Be ye not futtered enough?"

"Nay; that's not it. This one I loved ere I ever met Bza."

"So what think ye? To snatch this woman out of Orlandus' grasp and fetch her hither?'' Wok gave a rumbling chuckle. "We cavil not at a man's having more than one mate. Forsooth, it takes a real man—'' Wok thumped his furry chest with the sound of a bass drum "—to ride more than one at a time. I know. If they quarrel, he must needs make peace amongst them. If they act in concert, they nag him, one after another, until he gives in to their desire. If ye fetch your lowland sweetling hither, it will be a sight for the ancestral spirits how ye fare betwixt the twain.''

Thinking, Thorolf gnawed. "Not sure am I yet what stratagems would further my sire's bill to benefit the trolls.'' The horrid idea that had been lurking at the back of his mind could no longer be denied. Taking a deep breath, he said: "Could some troll guide me through the tunnel under Zurshnitt, so that I shall discover whither it leads and where it gives access to the world above?''

After a gulp and a belch, Wok replied: "Very well. I shall send Gak.''

Not only to guide me, thought Thorolf, but also to watch lest I turn against the trolls.

Ahead of the hillock on which stood Thorolf and Gak, the Venner Valley sprawled, in the misty midst of which lay Zurshnitt. Beyond the city rose the snow summits of the Dorblentz Range. Thorolf could just make out the dark protuberance in the middle of Zurshnitt that was Castle Hill and its fortlet.

"Go back down," grunted Gak, pointing down the slope away from the city. He stepped off the crest and skidded down the steep incline, checking his slide with the butt of his spear.

Thorolf, wearing the yellow robe he had taken from the dead Sophonomist spy, scrambled after. Gak halted at the base of a mossy outcrop of stone, forming a small cliff. The face of the outcrop was masked by a screen of creepers dangling from the bank above.

131

Gak's sky-blue eyes peered out from under his shaggy, overhanging brows. "Be sure nobody see," he growled.

He pushed the creepers aside, laid a hairy hand against the stone, and pushed. Groaning, a section of stone revolved about its vertical axis until the slab stood perpendicular to the face of the outcrop, half in and half out of the tunnel entrance.

Gak took a last look about and entered the hidden door. "Come!" he said in a stage whisper.

Thorolf took a deep breath, squared his shoulders, and fought his rising panic. He told himself: Come on, weren't you just as frightened when the howling mob of Tzenrican revolutionaries rushed upon you?

"What matter?" said Gak from within the tunnel. "Fear?"

At least, thought Thorolf, he could not let this backward aboriginal see that he was afraid. He forced himself to step boldly into the tunnel, ignoring the painful pounding of his heart.

"Dark!" he muttered.

"You see," said Gak. The troll slipped off his shoulder the strap of his goatskin bag. He took out a pair of rushlights and a Rhaetian copper igniter, and he charged the device with tinder.

"Where get?" asked Thorolf, pointing to the igniter.

"Trade. Soon we make, too." Gak pulled the trigger and lit the rushlights from the brief yellow flame. He handed one to Thorolf and pushed the door back to its closed position. The trolls, Thorolf saw, had cleverly fabricated the stone door to fit the tunnel entrance, with pivots at top and bottom.

The meager light enabled Thorolf to stride after Gak. The tunnel sloped down, leveled off, and sloped some more. Where the solid rock gave way to earth, the tunnel had been lined with rough-hewn planking. The planks overhead were braced at intervals by posts against collapse.

They walked and walked; when Thorolf's rushlight weakened, Gak produced another. The floor became wet. In places mud had worked its way up between the planks, giving a slippery surface on which the yellow flames of their torches cast a flickering reflection. Thorolf thought he could hear the rumble of street traffic overhead.

Little by little his panic subsided, only now and then returning with a rush. He smiled in the near-dark; if he would never really enjoy being in a tunnel, at least he could now face such burrows with becoming fortitude.

"Step!" muttered Gak.

Thorolf found that he was ascending a stair, then walking on a level, then climbing again. Now and then the opening of a side tunnel gaped blackly in the rush-light. The passage became so narrow that both Thorolf and Gak had to turn sideways to squeeze through. Thorolf fought down a return of panic.

"Quiet!" breathed Gak. Thorolf gripped his scabbard lest it clank or scrape against stone.

The tunnel ahead showed a feeble blur of gray against blackness. As they approached, Thorolf saw that the left-hand wall had been chiseled out to form a rectangular opening, large enough to go through without stooping but only a span deep. The far end was blocked by a screen of some sort, which admitted enough light for Thorolf's dark-adapted eyes to see.

As Thorolf peered at the screen, he picked out a variegated pattern of darker patches. The mottling resolved itself into a familiar-seeming form. Then he realized that he was looking at the back of a well-known painting. It was the huge picture, in the assembly chamber of the Rhaetian Senate, of Arnalt of Thessen, in armor, leading the charge against the Carinthians. To Thorolf's vision, the figures were reversed right and left.

Thorolf could not see anything in the room through the canvas. He listened, holding his breath, but detected no sounds of human presence. He gently touched the back of the painting. The canvas swung out and away a little; it was evidently hung from the top. A sharp hiss from Gak made him jerk his hand away, and the picture returned to its normal position with the ghost of a thump.

Thorolf wondered where the chimney flue led up from the fireplace over which the painting hung. By rights it should pass through the space where he now stood; but the masonry beneath his feet seemed solid. There must be an offset, carrying the flue beneath his feet to the passage wall behind him and then up. Perhaps the Carinthian governors had built these holes to spy upon the king's officials or to escape from Zurshnitt in a crisis.

Thorolf did not feel he could spend time on this architectural puzzle. "Now castle!" he whispered.

They went back to where the tunnel widened. Gak's light ahead seemed to vanish, leaving a faint afterglow. Hurrying, Thorolf found that the troll had turned into one of the side tunnels.

Again they walked and walked and climbed almost invisible stairs. The climb went on and on until even Thorolf, strong and inured to hardship though he was, found his breath coming faster. They wormed through passages even narrower than that which led to the Senate chamber.

At last Gak stopped, holding up a hand. Thorolf found that he faced another rectangle of dark gray against the blackness. This aperture was smaller than that into the Senate chamber but still large enough to squeeze through.

"Quiet!" murmured Gak. "Castle. Sophonomists here."

Thorolf examined the screen. The paint must be thicker on this picture, he thought; or else the light in the room beyond must be dimmer. He could not decipher the painting until he noticed several black patches against the gray, each in the form of an oak leaf. Then he remembered the painting of the Divine Couple in the Chamber of Audience, whither Orlandus had conducted him on his first visit to the Sophonomist lair. The black spots were the oak leaves that a later artist had painted to conceal the deities' sexual parts, in deference to the Rhaetians' puritanism.

There was, however, a tiny spot of light high up on the back of the painting; Thorolf remembered that the picture was slightly torn. He leaned forward and put his eye to the tear. By moving slightly he found that he could bring most of the chamber into view. The room seemed empty.

"Finish?" Gak asked. "Come away?"

Thorolf wagged a hand. "Wait!" he whispered. "Must see Sophonomists."

"Bad!" muttered Gak. "Have magic. Find us. . . ." Gak drew a finger across his throat.

"Fear?" asked Thorolf. Gak had put the same question to him at the tunnel entrance.

"No fear," said Gak rapping his chest with his knuckles. "No damn fool, either."

"Wait. . . ."

Thorolf stiffened at the sound of voices. One of the doors swung gently open. In came Yvette of Grintz, in a yellow robe, followed by the stout, red-haired, red-robed Parthenius, whom Thorolf had met before. The Countess was saying in that toneless deltaic voice:

". . . but my good Doctor, I must obey the Master's orders, and he has not commanded me to lie with you."

"But," expostulated Parthenius, "ye know I be Orlandus' second in command, his lieutenant in all things. Aught I ask, ye may take as coming from him. Since he cares not for commerce with women, 'tis nought to him whose bed ye haunt. So take this as an order, my lady: Ye shall repair to my chamber after curfew, to pass the night there in pleasure. Ye shall not regret it!"

"My pleasure is but to do my Master's will," said Yvette's flat voice. "Natheless, I will not comply without a direct command from the Master."

"Then bide ye here; I'll fetch our Psychomagus in person!"

"If he say so—" began Yvette; but Parthenius bustled out.

Thorolf's mind was in a whirl. The sight of Yvette aroused his passions to a feverish pitch. Parthenius' crude effort to extort her sexual favors filled him with blinding rage.

For the moment, the fact that Yvette was no gentle maiden but an experienced woman of the world mattered not at all. Thorolf wanted to get her out of Zurshnitt at any cost. What he would do with her, since she still acted as mechanically as one of the figurines that marked the hours on Rhaetian clocks, he had not figured out. He would get her away and let the future unfold as it would.

Thorolf pushed the back of the painting. Like the picture in the Senate chamber, this work of art was secured at the upper edge, so that it swung away from the wall. He pushed it farther and lowered himself to the floor, a little over a yard below the lower edge of the hole in the wall. Below the bottom of the picture the unused fireplace gaped; its chimney must follow the same zigzag route up as that in the Senate chamber.

As Thorolf gathered himself up and let the painting swing back, he heard a squawk from Gak: "Ho! Come back, fool!"

Yvette turned and stared at Thorolf, bringing her hand to her mouth with a jerky intake of breath. "Sergeant!" she cried, her blue eyes wide. "What dost?"

Thorolf bounded forward, reaching for her wrist. "Come, Yvette! I'll whisk you out of this prison!"

She backed away, avoiding his grasp. "I serve only the Master!" she said. Then she turned and fled toward the door through which Parthenius had vanished.

A thump behind Thorolf told him that Gak had also dropped into the room. The troll roared: "You crazy? Back!"

A glance showed Thorolf that Gak was rushing upon him with clutching hands. In quick succession, the three raced through the door and down the corridor beyond. Simultaneously, the scarlet-robed Orlandus and Parthenius appeared at the far end. Both gaped at the sight of Yvette, Thorolf, and Gak rushing toward them in single file, each trying to seize his predecessor.

"Who be you?" Parthenius shouted at Thorolf.

"He's no diaphane!" cried Orlandus. "He's a mundane disguised! That's a stolen robe!"

Yvette dodged past the leaders of Sophonomy. Thorolf, thinking that here was a chance to behead this evil cult at a blow, swept out his sword. The unarmed cultists should be easy prey.

Parthenius shouted: "Guards! To us!" Orlandus hurled something to the floor and shouted words. Instantly there appeared, between Thorolf and the Sophonomists, the fearsome figure of an ogre. It was half again as tall as a man, with a thick, warty hide. Webbed fingers and toes ended in talons, and a pair of horns surmounted pointed ears. From beneath its blob of a nose, like a weird mustache, sprang a pair of yard-long tendrils, which writhed like serpents. Looking sharply, Thorolf perceived that the ogre was slightly transparent. Bardi's anti-illusion spell was evidently still working.

Thorolf heard a yelp of dismay from Gak, who hurled his spear, turned, and ran back the way he had come. The spear went through the ogre and clattered on the floor beyond.

The ogre spread its taloned hands as if to seize Thorolf, who instinctively struck forehand with his sword. The blade passed through the torose body without resistance, so that the force of Thorolf's blow spun him round and almost felled him. Seeing Gak rushing through the door to the audience chamber, he shouted:

"Come back! 'Tis mere illusion!"

Gak continued his flight. Hearing the clatter of approaching guards, Thorolf ran after the troll.

When Thorolf reëntered the Chamber of Audience, Gak was disappearing into the passage behind the painting. Thorolf slammed the door behind him, shot the bolt, and pushed the divan in front of the door. Leaning toward the door, he shouted in Rhaetian:

"Out the other door, Gak! It leads to the main gate!"

Then he, too, pulled the painting out from the wall and hoisted himself into the dark aperture. From the blocked door came shouts and hammering.

Gak had picked up the two rushlights, which he had left leaning against the wall. He handed one to Thorolf, growling: "Quick, fool!"

The troll's big, hairy feet slapped the floor of the tunnel as he led the way with reckless haste. When they reached the junction with the main tunnel, they paused to catch their breath. Thorolf listened but heard nothing save his and Gak's heavy breathing. When their chests had ceased to heave, Gak said:

"You mad? Evil spirit have you?"

"My first mate," Thorolf gasped.

After a long pause, Gak said: "Ah! Understand. Come."

Back at the troll village, Thorolf told Wok of his adventure. Wok said: "Ye are lucky to escape the results of your folly at the cost of one spear. I will not let Gak or any other of my folk take part in another such foray. Too risky."

"It behooved me to do *something*," said Thorolf defensively.

"Wherefore? One lowland female more or less, what matter? I know not what ye see in lowland females anyway. Hideous, hairless, starved-looking creatures."

"Tastes differ," said Thorolf. "Anyway, Gak and I have found how you and your warriors can invade the

Sophonomist stronghold and destroy this menace once and for all.''

"Eh? Ye mean for us to trail through the tunnels and pop out of the hole behind that picture? Never! Those magicians would blast us with their spells. If those failed, their armored guards would fall upon us. We should be lucky if any got away alive. Besides, they probably know about the tunnel now and will have blocked it, or at least placed guards at the entrance.''

"I doubt that. I called out a misdirection ere they broke into the Chamber of Audience, to send them out the other door as if we had fled by the main gate. Gak and I heard no pursuit in the tunnel.''

"Ah! But Orlandus is clever. When the gate guards said none had passed them, he would know ye had left some other way and command a search, if indeed he have not already discovered the tunnel by his magical arts.''

Thorolf argued some more, trying to arouse in the Chief an eagerness to raid the Sophonomist headquarters and slaughter the lot—except Yvette, of course. But Wok remained adamant.

"Too much risk," he said. "We can fight you feeble, hairless lowlanders on even terms; but we have no magic like unto yours. At the bruit of the battle, your soldiers might come to investigate. When they saw the Sophonomists fighting us whom they deem beasts, they would join in against us. We are a small people and cannot afford to lose men.

"Besides, your lowland female might be slain. Even if I told my warriors to spare her, in the confusion they would strike at every yellow robe. Ye lowlanders all look alike to us.''

Thorolf sighed and gave up; but during the following days his resolution crystallized to make his next démarche against Sophonomy alone. The last time, he had impulsively plunged in without proper precautions and had accomplished nothing save to alert the cultists against intrusion. He was lucky to have escaped intact, and Gak had been right to call him a fool.

Since Thorolf was not normally impulsive, he wondered at his own rashness. It must, he thought, be a case of the power of love. Doctor Vipsanio at Genuvia had spoken of the crazy deeds into which love can lead one. Thorolf resolved that next time, he would leave nothing more to chance than he could help. He began by sending another letter to his father.

On the appointed day, when the light powdering of an early snow was melting off the ground, he found the consul seated on a folding chair beside their special pool and fishing. But Zigram was not alone. With him on another stool sat Chief Constable Lodar.

Thorolf hesitated, wondering if they meant to arrest him. To reassure himself, he scouted stealthily around, using all the skills that his soldierly experience and his sojourn among the trolls had taught him. He discovered five guards, sitting in a hollow near their tethered horses and casting dice.

Well, he thought, if they should try to spring a surprise, he could probably outrun the lot, since he was younger than either Zigram or Lodar and not laden with mail like the guards. Taking a deep breath, he stepped out from behind the same spruce sapling that had concealed Yvette on their first meeting.

"Hail!" he said.

"Kernun's toenails!" cried Zigram, dropping his fishing rod. "Startle me not so, son! Wherefore have ye dragged us elders up here now?"

"Information," said Thorolf. "Am I wanted for Bardi's death?"

"Only as a witness; and Gunthram hath posted your name as absent without leave. When the Carinthian rascals found some hedge-wizard to open Bardi's chest, one got drunk on his share of the loot and boasted he'd buy a dukedom. He was heard in a tavern; so he's in durance awaiting the rope; whilst his mates, we presume, have fled back to Carinthia.

"The constables scoured the countryside, seeking a hunchback who, calling himself Bardi's apprentice, was thought to have been either Bardi's slayer or your confederate in the deed; but the Carinthian's boast disproved that surmise.

"When come ye back to answer the justicers' questions and resume your post? We are not fain to hang the rascal until we have your tale to complete the puzzle with the final piece. I've told Colonel Gunthram ye fled at my command, to look into a plot against the Commonwealth and that, therefore, ye be liable to no penalties. Methinks he believed me not, but he durst not call me liar to my face."

"You mentioned that the last time we met," said Thorolf. "But what news of Sophonomy? I am sure the Commonwealth has a spy amongst Orlandus' guards."

Zigram and Lodar exchanged glances. The Chief Constable spoke: "Daily their influence grows. Methinks at least a third of my constables be under Orlandus' thumb. When one of their folk is brought to book, they frighten judges, juries, and witnesses into inaction, letting the miscreants go free."

The Consul added: "A curious tale hath come to our ears, Thorolf. It is that, within the past fortnight, Orlandus and his deputy, an old mountebank and street fighter calling himself Doctor Parthenius, encountered your Countess fleeing along a corridor in the castle, pursued by you and a troll. The Psychomage, who knew you not at once, warded off your attack by a spell, whereupon ye twain—ye and the troll—utterly vanished. Although all exits are guarded, none saw you emerge; nor did a search of the edifice discover you.

"Orlandus concluded that ye had employed a spell of invisibility, like unto that on the spy he sent to follow me hither. So he hath devised a kind of blower, like that wherewith we spray our flowers to ward off snails.

He hath ordered a hundred of these devices from Grimbald the sheet-metal worker and plans to charge them with flour. If ye seek to haunt his castle unseen, he'll spray you with this powder, thus making your presence patent.''

'' 'Tis a trifle cold to run about naked at this season,'' Thorolf said. ''But why asked he not the Countess? She knows how I gained access to's stronghold, and the spirit possessing her would have compelled her to answer true.''

''Another mystery, son. He did so question her, we are told, whereupon she was stricken with muteness. Not a word hath she spoken since.''

''Some spell!'' said Thorolf. ''Yvette normally talks as a horse gallops.''

''Like that fellow in Helmanax's play who saith a woman who keeps on talking can always get her way, eh? Our informant reports that Orlandus contemplates torture to wring the true answers from her. Forsooth, how gat ye into that pile and out again?''

Thorolf grinned. ''When Sophonomy be expunged, I'll tell you all. Meanwhile I'm happy to learn you have able spies in the castle. Double-bolt your doors of nights, and farewell!''

Again, Thorolf stood before the little creeper-masked cliff concealing the tunnel entrance. This time he had come with his pack well laden, trying to anticipate every contingency. He glanced at the sun, hanging low on the mountain peaks. Since he planned to invade the castle at night, he sat and ate, killing time to wait for darkness.

At last he rose, brushed crumbs from his hands, and pushed open the stony door. He paused at the entrance; his old panic surged back. Sweat beaded his brow despite the near-freezing temperature. Then he thought of Yvette's slender members stretched on some infernal

device, while Orlandus hovered, murmuring in his ole-
aginous voice:

"Now, my dear, you need only answer a few simple
questions. . . ."

Thorolf squared his jaw and marched into the cavity.
He paused to ignite a rushlight from his pack, to close
the door behind him, and to change from his heavy
boots to goatskin slippers, which he himself had made
to enable himself to move in silence.

Thorolf lost time by mistakenly entering a wrong side
tunnel but finally found the opening to the Chamber of
Audience in Zurshnitt Castle. Looking through the tear
in the canvas, he saw that the room was dimly lit by a
single candle. He watched, he estimated, a full half-
hour. Nobody entered the chamber.

The candle burned slowly down; in another hour it
would gutter out. Thorolf would never let one of his
soldiers forget a burning candle! Such carelessness
risked a conflagration; besides, candles cost money,
which the colonel had to extract, with much effort, from
the Senate and ultimately from the Rhaetian taxpayers.

Thorolf dropped his pack on the floor, cast off his
cloak, and unrolled a bundle of yellow cloth. This was
the robe of the dead invisible diaphane. He put on the
robe, pulled the hood over his head, and lowered himself through the opening.

The painting swung back; Thorolf caught it before it
struck the wall and let it gently complete its swing. For
an instant he stood on the balls of his feet, listening.
The only sounds were the tramp of sentries on the foot-
walk atop the outer wall, punctuated by challenges and
passwords. He thought he could hear a snore, but the
sound was too faint to be sure of.

He slowly drew his sword. The blade came silently,
because he had stuffed pinches of moss into the scabbard. He bolted the left-hand door and stepped to the
door on the right. This, if his sketch was correct, should

lead to the row of cubicles that included Yvette's bed-chamber.

When he opened the door to the corridor parallel to that wherein he had chased Yvette the other time, the hall stretched dimly away. At the far end, a wall bracket supported a little lamp, the feeble light of which cast yellow highlights on the metal door handles. Behind those doors, presumably, slept the upper ranks of the diaphanes.

Thorolf stole down the corridor almost to its end. He counted the doors on his right; there were twelve. At the eleventh he halted; if he had his directions straight, this should be Yvette's room.

He gently tried the door handle. It turned with a mousey squeak. Thorolf peered into the crack and found the room in darkness.

On tiptoe, Thorolf let himself in, leaving the door a little ajar to furnish light. The cubicle was tiny; the bed, a small night table, a chair, and a little wardrobe left hardly space for the occupant to move about. Thorolf froze at the discovery that the bed was empty.

He bent, groping for the pillow. The bed had been occupied since it was last made. Thorolf laid his sword on the bed and sat down, thinking. After a moment he rose and examined the wardrobe. The room was certainly Yvette's. There hung, among other garments, the beaded golden gown she had worn on their aborted assignation at the Green Dragon.

Thinking she had possibly risen to visit the jakes, Thorolf sat back on the bed and waited. After half an hour, he was sure that she had departed on some other errand. Could it be that Parthenius had persuaded Orlandus to bend her to his lustful desires? The very thought infuriated Thorolf; but after his previous raid he had better sense than to go charging about the castle at random, sword in hand.

Another half-hour passed before he heard soft foot-steps outside. In came Yvette in a nightrobe and dressing gown, carrying a candlestick whose candle shed a cheerful yellow glow across the unmade bed. When she saw Thorolf she halted, staring blankly.

Thorolf sprang up. With a sweeping motion he grabbed the candlestick, blew out the candle, and tossed the holder on the bed. Then he caught Yvette by the shoulders, whirled her around, and clapped a hand over her mouth.

She bit his hand, causing him to release his grip for an instant; but instead of uttering a shriek for help she emitted only an inarticulate, "Mmm! Mmm!"

He had come prepared to gag her; but apparently this would not be needed, since she still was under the spell of muteness. Like a frightened animal she tried to punch and scratch him. But he pinned her slender arms, retrieved his sword, and hustled her out. He dragged her at a near-run the length of the corridor and into the Chamber of Audience. As he closed and bolted the door behind him, Yvette struggled silently to break free.

He faced a problem. To hold the picture out from the wall and boost the Countess into the aperture, he would need both hands and some coöperation. But if he released her, she would try to run to Orlandus and thwart his efforts at abduction.

At last he sheathed his sword and brought out of the pocket in his robe a strip of cloth with which he had meant to bind or gag Yvette. He held her slender wrists in the grip of one broad hand, bound the cloth around them, and released her, holding the free end as she continued to strain away from him.

Through the left-hand door Orlandus called: "Open up, here!"

Thorolf hauled Yvette over to the picture and pulled it out from the wall. But how to get his recalcitrant victim into the hole?

Holding the picture away from the wall with his head, he clamped both hands on her slender waist, preparatory to heaving her up and in. Then he heard the sounds of a chant, followed by the clank of a withdrawn bolt.

Thorolf whirled. In the doorway stood Orlandus in a nightrobe, below which his shanks and feet were bare and above which his scalp was bald save for a narrow fringe of mouse-colored hair. Evidently the Psychomage was wizard enough to force a door to unbolt itself, even if not enough to grow hair on his pate, which Thorolf had always seen concealed beneath a wig of glossy black.

"Who the devil—" began the Psychomagus, starting forward. Then he checked. "Sergeant Thorolf again, I see. And wearing one of our habits!"

Thorolf's attention was distracted long enough for Yvette to whirl out of his grasp and run toward Orlandus, trailing the strip of cloth by which Thorolf had tried to control her.

As the Countess approached Orlandus, the cultist threw an arm around her. With his other hand he whisked a dagger out of his robe and placed the edge against her throat.

"Yield!" said Orlandus. "Or your jade's dinner for my hounds!"

Thorolf measured the distance between himself and the pair. He could doubtless whip out his sword, cross the distance in two bounds, and smite Orlandus to earth. But it would take even less time for the Psychomagus to slash open that slender neck.

"Throw down your sword, scabbard and all, unless you're fain to see her weazand slit!" barked Orlandus.

Thorolf hesitated, frantically weighing alternatives. Then he took the one that seemed to offer the likeliest chance. He hoisted his baldric over his head and, stooping, laid the belt and scabbard on the floor, at the same time easing his dagger from its sheath.

When he straightened up, the dagger was in his right hand, away from Orlandus. It was a sizable weapon, weighted for throwing, and he threw. The fact that Orlandus was a full head taller than Yvette gave Thorolf a reasonable target.

He hoped to drive the blade into the magician's eye. Instead the dagger, turning in its flight, buried itself in Orlandus' shoulder. The mage's right arm sagged, and his dagger clattered to the floor.

Thorolf scooped up his scabbarded sword, drew, and leaped toward his enemy. The cultist, releasing Yvette to reach for his dagger with his unwounded arm, cried:

"Hold! Be reasonable, man! Think of what I offer you—"

As he spoke, Orlandus abandoned his quest for his dagger and, beginning an incantation, backed hastily away from the charging Thorolf. Unaware of his direction, the cultist backed, not out the door, but into the frame of one of the diamond-paned windows. The casement flew open at the impact of the magician's shoulders, and Orlandus fell out backward. Thorolf glimpsed the mage's bare feet inverted and heard a hoarse cry. Then came the sound of a body striking the bailey below.

Thorolf put his head out the window. He could see nothing in the darkness; but the cry and the thud of the fall had alerted the guards on the outer wall. One called:

"What was that? . . . Let us go down for a look. . . ."

Yvette stood with her hands still bound behind her, looking dazed. Thorolf said: "Are you free from the spell, Countess?"

She stared at him but made no answer.

Evidently she was not yet free. Thorolf sheathed his blade, donned his baldric, and carried Yvette over to the picture. This time he hoisted her, unhelpful but unresisting, into the tunnel and scrambled after her. As the picture swung back into place, shouts and clatter of armed men came through the canvas, together with a curious intermittent hiss, like the sound of a monster breathing.

Thorolf knew he should flee without pause, but his curiosity proved too great. Placing his eye to the tear in the canvas, he saw two of Orlandus' mailed guards glancing wildly about the room. One, just then peering under the divan, bore a halberd; the other carried a cylindrical device with a handle at one end, while the other end tapered to a slender orifice. The guard was rhythmically pulling the handle out and pushing it back in. With each push, a pillowy puff of flour spouted from the orifice. The clouds of flour dust rapidly fogged the room until vision was useless.

Smiling quietly, Thorolf picked up his pack and cloak and herded Yvette down the tunnel.

IX
The Disappearing Delta

Thorolf lay close beside Yvette in the darkness of his little tent, which accommodated two sleepers only by crowding. The cold compelled them to sleep in their clothes, he in his Sophonomist robe and she in her nightwear, with his cloak over both.

Once they were out of sight of Zurshnitt, he unbound her hands, warning her that, if she tried to flee back to Castle Hill, she would get lost and perish. She had obeyed in a dazed sort of way, as if Orlandus' death had robbed her of all volition. Thorolf could understand how her delta became quiescent when its sorcerermaster was no longer present to command it; but still he was wary. The spirit might force Yvette to do something utterly unpredictable.

When they retired, Thorolf had tied up his sword with his scarf and lain down upon the bundle, so that Yvette could not draw the weapon without arousing him. His dagger had gone out the window with Orlandus.

The lumpy bundle, together with the cold, made sleep hard to come by, despite the fact that the night had been well along towards dawn before Thorolf halted their flight to set up the tent. A nasty little thought kept stealing into his mind: If he tried to futter her now, she would probably not resist, at least not hard or long. Feeling ashamed of himself, Thorolf banished the idea; but it kept creeping back.

He was lying in the dark, concocting and discarding plans for taking care of Yvette until she was restored, when he became aware of a faint illumination that was not dawnlight. A little twinkling point of blue light, like that of a firefly, appeared over Yvette's face. It rose, danced about for a few heartbeats, then streaked out the crack in the tent flap.

Thorolf raised himself on one elbow to watch the apparition's progress. The movement aroused Yvette, who sat up crying: "Where am I?"

"In my tent," said Thorolf, "on our way to the Sharmatt Range."

"Your voice doth sound familiar—are you Sergeant Thorolf?"

"The same, madam." He gathered himself to rise. "Let me strike a light."

Soon he had a rushlight sending up its feeble flame. Yvette reached out and touched his face. "I do perceive that you are in sooth Thorolf! I recall your taking me from Castle Zurshnitt when something befell the Psychomagus; but all is confused. Is he dead?"

"I have reason to think so. And the delta that possessed you, left masterless, has departed your body."

"Ah, it all comes back! To you I owe my liberation; you are a true hero even if a Rhaetian." She seized his head between her hands and kissed him. "A pity you are of your class, or I should know how truly to reward you. And now I can talk again!"

150

"Why couldn't you before?"

"When the Master asked me how you escaped from the castle, my delta would have answered; whilst I stood firm against exposing the secret, lest you essay another rescue and be trapped. So bitter was this opposition internal that I found myself stricken dumb. How came you to my chamber so timely? By the tunnel again?"

"I followed the sketch of the interior made under your direction. Finding the room empty, I sat down to await your return."

"I was with that beast Parthenius."

"So I feared. Did he—ah—you and he were disputing the matter when I broke in before."

"Aye, nor did he abandon his quest. But today, at his behest, Orlandus commanded my delta to obey Parthenius; so tonight I did attend him."

"How—I mean, was it? . . ." Embarrassed, Thorolf let his voice trail off.

"Did he pleasure me, mean you? Never! He is brutal and insatiable; after three bouts he finally fell asleep and I slipped away, or he'd be at it yet. A troll were a meeter lover."

"Poor dear!" said Thorolf, whose mind was running on the reward Yvette said she would have given him had he only a little noble blood. Her tale gave him a mixture of disappointment and relief. He had long fantasized about making love to her, if he haled her away from the castle and got rid of her delta. But his anticipation was qualified by a tiny fear that she would make some scathing comment, comparing him to one or another of her former lovers. He therefore felt some relief at having their relationship settled for the time being. Perhaps his father was right in warning him away from titled ladies.

Yvette said: "And you are the lad who cared nought for rescuing maidens—or at least ladies—from vile enchanters! Now tell me all that has befallen!" She spoke briskly, fast resuming her old authoritarian self.

When Thorolf had recounted Bardi's magical blunder, she put in: "I should like to pull out that old fool's whiskers, hair by hair!"

"You can't. Bardi is dead."

"How so?"

"Some of Duke Gondomar's men slew him as they robbed his house."

"Oh, the poor old dodderer! Now tell me whither we are bound, and to what end?"

Thorolf told how he had sought refuge among the trolls. "But there's a complication." He reported his forced wedding to Bza, and his leaving his marital duties to Bza's lover Khop.

"It matters not," said Yvette, "since neither this Bza nor I has any wish to wed you."

"I hope no trouble arise from that matter. I apologize in advance for the village. You'll find a troll settlement a foul sort of place."

"One of my rank," she snapped, "can take the rough with the smooth. Only the lower classes expect things to go on lifelong without change." She paused. "And then what next, my good Sergeant? I trust you expect me not to pass my life amongst trolls!"

"Of course not! But I have not yet decided upon a plan. If Orlandus be dead, perchance the spines of government will stiffen enough to seize the castle and bring those within to book. Orlandus' use of deltas would support a list of indictments as long as your arm."

She sniffed. "Always your cautious Rhaetian legalisms! A true hero would round up a band of followers, seize the castle, slaughter the miscreants, and let the lawyers argue legality. That is what I should have done had they obtained a foothold in Grintz."

"So indeed would I, were I sure that more good than evil would flow from the deed. But we Rhaetians know that, if it's the practice to take the law into one's own hands, the winner will be the most faithless and ruthless, be he never such a villain."

"A true knight would act first and then ponder the ifs and buts—''

"Oh, go to sleep! You'd liefer argue than eat, and we have two days' walk ahead of us.''

The sun was well up when, fatigued as they were, they at last woke up for good. Thorolf served Yvette an austere breakfast of hardtack and trollish beer, the latter slightly improved by straining it through a clean sock before jugging it. Although Yvette's face registered distaste, she downed the repast without verbal complaint.

When they set out, they went more slowly than Thorolf had expected because Yvette could not keep up with his walking pace. Moreover, her bedroom slippers soon began to wear out on the rough pathways. They stopped in midmorning while Thorolf dug his goatskin slippers out of the pack. These proved so much too large for her that they came off at every step.

At last he got out his spare socks and put them on over her bedroom slippers, tying them in place with one of the strips of cloth he had brought to bind and gag her.

When they resumed, Yvette paused where the trail ran through a muddy patch. "Ugh!" she said. "Your socks will be full of mud, unless we climb around.''

"The socks will be done for by the time we reach the village in any case. This is a little-used path the trolls revealed me. Here, I'll carry you.''

He picked her up and started across. Halfway he paused, staring at the ground. "What is't?'' she asked.

"An interesting track, and recent.'' He stepped to one side and stood Yvette on a small boulder. "Stand for a trice whilst I study it.''

"Oh, come on! Wouldst waste the day trailing beasts?''

Thorolf ignored the comment. "Here's a man in proper mountain boots, and here we have two—nay, three others—in common shoon, apparently following him.''

"How know you which came first?''

"Because here, and again here, one of the trio stepped on the print of the booted man.''

He picked her up again and bore her to the end of the slough. She asked: "Were those following the booted man, or did they come by long after?''

"That I cannot tell.'' Later, he paused where the path forked, pointing to footprints on the right-hand path. "Thither went that dubious quartet. Our path lies to the left, but methinks I'll make a cast along the right-hand path to ascertain whither it leads.''

"Nay, do not so! I wish to reach this trollish village forthwith; I tire.''

Thorolf gave Yvette a hard look. "Harken, Countess; we've been through this before. I'll investigate this matter as I see fit—''

"You shall not! Your first duty is to me!''

"Rubbish, my dear Yvette! You're not my feudal suzerain. Abide at the fork or come with me, as you like; the latter were safer.''

Thorolf started off on the right-hand fork. Yvette waited until he had gone a few steps, then hurried after him, muttering: "Whoreson knotpate! Incondite ass! Defying thy betters like a god-detested revolutionary—''

Thorolf turned his head to say: "Oh, shut up! To a free Rhaetian, no one's a better.''

She subsided. Thorolf tramped ahead, scanning the ground for tracks. After half an hour he held up a cautionary hand, whispering:

"Something's up, ahead! Be very quiet!''

"But—''

"I said *quiet*! Must I gag you?''

Cautiously they advanced. In a small depression in the path ahead, three armed men had Doctor Berthar, the director of the Zoölogical Park in Zurshnitt, backed against a boulder. Holding weapons against his chest and throat, they were relieving him of any detachable possessions.

Thorolf searched among the stones beside the path and found one a little larger than one of his own fists. He breathed: "Stay here whilst I fordo those rogues!"

"But three, and at least one in mail! If you lose, what of me?"

"Flee back to Zurshnitt and take refuge with my father, the Consul. I have my reasons."

Without further words, Thorolf drew his sword. Holding the hilt in his left hand and the stone in his right, he stalked quietly toward the group in the hollow. So quietly did he move and so intent were the robbers on their victim that he was a mere dozen yards away when one of them cried: "Ho! Look around!"

Thorolf broke into a run until, a few feet from the group, he hurled his stone at the mailed swordsman. The rock struck the side of the man's head and flung him sprawling in the herbage.

Thorolf shifted his sword to his right hand and bored in. He faced one man with a sword and one with a long dagger, neither apparently mailed. He attacked the swordsman with a tremendous backhand slash. It was not the skilled swordplay of which Thorolf was capable; but he did it advisedly—and what he hoped for happened. The man easily parried, but the other's lighter weapon broke at the impact of Thorolf's heavier blade.

The man threw the stump of his sword at Thorolf, who ducked. Then both robbers fled along the trail. Thorolf ran after them; but they steadily widened the gap between them and their pursuer. Breathing hard, Thorolf came back to where Berthar was gathering up the loot that the robbers had dropped.

"Thorolf!" exclaimed Berthar. "I never expected rescue. If ever I take my seat on the Board, you shall have an appointment for the asking. 'Twere useless for me to fight at those odds."

Thorolf bent over the fallen man, who was beginning to revive. Thorolf put the point of his sword to the man's throat, saying: "Correct me if I err, sirrah, but methinks you're one of those rascals sent by the Duke of Landai, who assailed my father and me on the banks of the Rissel last month. Did Gondomar also command you to rob honest citizens of Rhaetia?"

When the man merely glared in silence, Thorolf pushed his sword a little harder. "Ouch!" said the man. "If I answer, will you then slay me?"

"Nay. I promise not to—this time, anyway—an your replies be truthful. I know enough of your doings to catch you in lies. Swink you still for the Duke?"

"Nay. We decided in council to quit his service."

"After you took the old wizard's treasure chest. Why didst kill poor old Bardi?"

" 'Twas not I but Ragned who cut his throat, whilst Offo held him. He'd begun to mutter some spell. Had we not killed him, he had conjured up some demon or monster to slay us instead."

"After you killed him, what then?"

"We agreed it were more profitable to divide the loot and go our ways than to go on risking our lives for this niggardly Duke. Besides, we and our comrades had thrice failed in our efforts to capture that countess with whom he's besotted, and his Pomposity would have taken a fourth failure ill indeed."

"How gat you the chest open, since it was locked by a magical spell?"

"We took it to one of your Zurshnitt magicians," said the robber.

"Which? Methinks I know, but tell me natheless."

"Ouch! Pray, stop prodding me with that thing. 'Twas Doctor Avain."

"Thought so. There were seven of you. What's befallen the others?"

"When we divided the contents, Lodovic accused our captain, Cheldimus, of cheating him, and Cheldimus stabbed Lodovic. That left six to share. Cheldimus took his portion and vanished, saying he was bound for Tyrrhenia to buy an estate and retire. Something about beating's hanger into a plowshare. Ragned got drunk and boasted, so the constables took him. I ween he's been hanged.''

''Not yet but soon. Go on!''

''That left Offo. His pelf was stolen by a whore he bedded; I know not whither he went.''

''And the surviving trio?''

''Alas! Drink and gambling and whoring frittered away our fortunes at a rate ye could scarce believe. Ere we knew, we were down to our last few coins. We durst not return to Landai, for the Duke would hang us for flouting his commands. So here we are—or at least, here am I. Now, wilt abide your promise to let me live?''

''Aye,'' said Thorolf, ''for now. If I meet you again, you're a dead man. But first I'll collect a small bounty, as you were doing to Doctor Berthar. Take his weapons and purse, Berthar; and pull off that mail shirt and hood. . . . We can use those good boots, too. Give me his dagger, pray; I lost mine.''

Berthar unclasped the gold-and-garnet brooch that held the robber's cloak. ''Ho!'' cried the robber. ''Take not my cloak, I beg; or I shall freeze to death on these cold nights!''

''I will let him keep his cloak,'' said Berthar. ''But one of those who fled got away with my good clasp; so I'll keep this one.''

Thorolf looked around to see Yvette approaching. He said: ''Madam, do you remember Doctor Berthar, of the Zoölogical Park?''

Berthar was struggling with the mail hood, the links of which had been driven by the stone into the flesh of the robber's cheek and ear. The Carinthian bled freely when the mesh was pulled away.

''I remember Doctor Berthar,'' Yvette said, ''though

my memories of the time I was possessed are vague and dreamy. Greetings, Doctor. Thorolf, I'm surprised that one as powerful as you failed to catch those twain.''

Thorolf grinned embarrassedly. "Running is not my strongest point.''

"No wonder, with that great mass of flesh! You should starve yourself down to slimness like unto mine. Then you could outrun such cullions.''

"Madam!'' said Thorolf. "That at which you cavil is not fat but solid thew. If you believe me not, I'll swing you round my head by the ankles to prove it, as I did with that soldier who jeered at my morals.''

"Doctor Berthar! Wilt stand by and let this gorbellied lob shend me with insults?''

"My dear Countess,'' said Berthar, "since he hath half mine age and twice my size, I see not what I can do about it. Certes, the sight of your Highness being whirled about thus were a robustious spectacle. He'd fling you into the next province.''

"Trust you men to hang together!'' she snapped.

"Anyway,'' said Thorolf, "nought incites a man to speed like a deadly foe in pursuit. You may doff my socks, Yvette, ere they crumble like last month's journey cake, and put this rogue's shoon on over yours. Methinks they're big enough.''

"I will also take his cloak,'' she said. "These flimsy nightclothes suffice me not in this clime.''

The captive started to protest, but a flourish of Thorolf's sword silenced him. Thorolf turned to Berthar. "What brings you into the Sharmatts?''

"A little red-and-black salamander,'' Berthar replied, "like unto that which you saw in my chamber. It lurks under stones by day. Now they'll be hibernating, and I hope to gather a few for my terraria.''

"Why should anyone,'' began Yvette in scornful tones, "take trouble over a tiny, wormy lizard—''

Berthar interrupted: "But this is a rare specimen, not hitherto known from this region! If these prove a new

158

species, I may have it named for me!'' He bent to peer at the prostrate Carinthian. ''Sirrah, be ye not one of the rogues who, essaying to kidnap Countess Yvette, delivered my dragon from his cage?''

''Well—ah—'' mumbled the man, ''we sought not to harm anyone; merely to create a diversion. . . .''

''Diversion!'' shouted Berthar. ''Risking the life of my priceless specimen! For that ye shall suffer the extremest penalty!''

Yvette spoke: ''Forsooth, Thorolf, what meanst to do with this knave?''

''I promised not to kill him; so I shall let him go.''

''What?'' cried Berthar. ''A mad idea! He should be haled back to Zurshnitt to stand trial for his felonies. It is the court's business whether to lengthen his neck or shorten it.''

''Nonsense!'' said Yvette. ''You'd make a pother over nought. Thorolf, all we need is one good slash, and we can bury the head and the body.''

''Not done in our orderly, legal manner, madam,'' said Berthar.

''Oh, futter your republican legalisms!'' she snapped. ''You idiot, the right thing is to kill him, and the sooner the better.''

''I cannot,'' said Thorolf. ''I promised, even though I owe him a debt for his part in my friend's murder. But to slay him now were dishonorable.''

''Honor! You?'' cried Yvette scornfully. ''There's no such thing in Rhaetia, since you have no nobles—not even knights. *I* could not slay him after promising life; but with you—''

''I have mine own code of honor—'' began Thorolf, but she rushed on:

''My dear Sergeant, persons of the lower classes have no concern with honor. As commoners go you're a fine fellow; but for you to prate of honor is like a frog lecturing on literary style.''

Thorolf snorted angrily; but Berthar spoke: ''The

L. Sprague de Camp & Catherine Crook de Camp

main thing is to assure a swift, just punishment; and that means—"

"And how wouldst get him to Zurshnitt by yourself?" asked Thorolf.

"Ye could hold him prisoner whilst I went to town and sent the constables—"

"You mean, stand over this wittol for a week? Be not absurd—"

"You're two hairsplitting noddies!" shrilled Yvette. "The only sane course—"

All three were shouting and gesticulating. While Thorolf's attention was distracted, the prisoner rolled suddenly to his feet and fled. Thorolf ran after him; but the man, though in stocking feet, ran like a deer. Thorolf gave up and returned, panting.

"See—see what happens when you engage in foolish disputes?" he gasped.

"Ye were disputing as loudly as any," growled Berthar. "To loose a villain who's harmed one of my animals—"

Yvette broke into a peal of laughter. "Confess, my good friends, we were all a pack of zanies! I still think I was right; but now the rascal hath settled the matter for us. 'Twere a scene from one of Helmanax's comedies. Let's be on our ways."

Thorolf and Berthar grinned shamefacedly. Thorolf asked: "We are bound for the village of the Sharmatt trolls; whither for you?"

Berthar thought. "If I may, I'll go with you. I know Chief Wok, and meseems it were safer with him then wending alone. I might meet those three seeking revenge."

"Fair enough. Take the rogue's sword."

Thorolf led the way back to the fork. Walking with Yvette, Berthar said: "Countess, today ye seem like a different person, compared to how ye were at the park. Then ye were as silent as a tomb."

160

"Oh, I can explain," said Yvette, launching into a voluble account of her captivity and rescue.

The delay meant an extra night of camping out before reaching the village. Thorolf and Berthar pooled their remaining food. When Yvette had stepped away for privacy, Berthar said:

"Your little Countess is amazing, Thorolf. Tell me, are ye and she—ah—well, betrothed or something of the sort?"

Thorolf frowned. "Nay, neither betrothed nor 'something of the sort.' To her Rhaetians are lower-class persons and hence ineligible. Why?"

"I did but wonder. 'Tis plain the pair of you know each other passing well; yet from the way ye squabble one would think you an old married couple."

"So far, Yvette's company has entailed many pains of the wedded state without the pleasures."

Staring into their little fire, Berthar said: "Since my whilom wife absconded, I've been alone. Your Countess mightily attracts me. Ye'll not mind?"

"N-no," said Thorolf. "But I warn you, she'll give your suit a rough reception."

When Yvette returned, she said: "Where wilt sleep, Doctor Berthar? The sergeant and I can barely fit into that little tent."

"I brought a sleeping sack," said Berthar, pulling it out of his pack. "It will suffice me."

"Thorolf!" said Yvette in her commanding voice. "Let you take the good Doctor's sack, whilst he and I occupy the tent!"

Startled, Thorolf said: "Well—ah—wherefore?"

"You're so thick of thew, there's in sooth room for but you in the tent. I must needs lie pressed against you, in dread that the great mass of muscle roll over and crush the life from me. I dream that I am but an insect upon whom your boot is descending. Berthar, being of sparer figure, would better fit." She wrinkled her nose. "Besides, I have reason to suspect you've not bathed lately."

"She makes sense," murmured Berthar, "but I would not dislodge you without your consent."

"Oh, fiddle-faddle!" cried Yvette. "I've stated my wishes!"

Thorolf felt the stirring of jealousy and of annoyance at being so rudely displaced. On the other hand, he did not wish to antagonize Berthar, who might some day help his reëntry into Academe. It was partly to conciliate Berthar that he had attacked the three Carinthians singlehanded. Besides, he admitted to himself that he must stink from his unwashedness.

"Oh, very well," he grumbled. "Do not mind Yvette's manner, Berthar. Betimes she confuses herself with Frea, the mother goddess of her Dualist Faith, and thinks all us mortals her subjects."

"Insolent jackanapes!" she said. Ignoring the comment, Thorolf crawled into the sleeping sack and watched unhappily as his companions fitted themselves into the tent.

Next morning, Thorolf was up and had the little fire going before Berthar and Yvette emerged from the tent, yawning and stretching mightily and grinning as if viewing Helmanax's hilarious masterpiece, *Mistress in Name Only*. The play had been banned in Zurshnitt as subversive of morality; but a group of players gave secret performances in a barn beyond the city limits.

Thorolf looked dourly at his companions. They had slept fully clad; but that was no insuperable obstacle. . . .

"Sleep well?" he snapped.

"Magnificent well!" said Yvette. " 'Twas as sound as in mine own palace. You were a dear to permit it!" She leaned over and kissed Thorolf's cheek. Sometimes, he thought, she acted almost human.

Through the day, the Countess and the park superintendent chattered, joked, and laughed in high good humor. Drawing inferences, Thorolf became ever more dour and silent.

A group of trolls stopped them, demanding tribute. Thorolf talked their way past this border guard, and the trio reached Wok's village in midafternoon.

The Chief came puffing up, crying: "Ah, good my Thorolf! And the learned Doctor Berthar! What seek ye this time? Worms or gnats?"

"A species of salamander—" began Berthar, but Wok ignored his reply, saying:

"Is this your other mate, Thorolf?"

"She is Countess Yvette of Grintz, from Carinthia. Countess, I present the mighty Chief Wok—"

"What this?" said Bza loudly in Trollish, pushing brusquely into the group. "No say can have other mate!"

"What's she grunting about?" asked Yvette.

"Well—ah—this is Bza, of whom I told you—"

"Want other mate, ask me first!" shouted Bza. "Me boss; her servant!"

Thorolf said: "She claims mastery over you, as senior wife—"

"I never heard of aught so ridiculous!" cried Yvette. "Tell this apish she-pig where to stick her wishes!"

"Bza!" said Thorolf in a soothing manner. "Listen! She no mate; just friend. Nobody boss—"

"Me know lowland word!" screamed Bza. "Me kill!"

Bza hurled herself at Yvette; the two came together in a shrieking whirl of golden hair. Bza was trying to tear out a double handful of Yvette's tresses, while the Countess fiercely punched and kicked her antagonist.

Thorolf cried: "Stop them, Wok!" He caught Bza from behind and whacked her knuckles with the hilt of the dagger he had taken from the Carinthian until she released Yvette's hair. Wok had seized Yvette around the waist and whirled her away from Bza. Thorolf turned Bza around and gave her a shove that sent her staggering away.

"Enough from you twain!" he shouted, sheathing his dagger. "No fight, Bza! Or me beat!"

"Limp lowlander, no can futter!" yelled Bza.

Before Thorolf could find further words, he felt his dagger snatched from its sheath. Next, Yvette was running at Bza, the dagger raised for a downward stab.

Thorolf hurled himself after the Countess, catching her just before she reached her victim. With the flying tackle he brought Yvette to earth. She rolled over, shrieking:

"Loon! Whoreson rudesby! Lickspittle! Roynish pajock! I'll teach thee to lay vile hands upon my princely person!"

She tried to stab Thorolf, who caught her wrist and twisted until she released the knife. Since the tirade continued, he slapped her, hard.

"Idiot!" he growled. "Want them to cut you up and boil you for dinner? That's what they do to bothersome lowlanders."

Yvette dissolved in tears. Thorolf added: "And next time you try to stab someone, hold the knife point up." He looked up to see a scowling Khop, Bza's lover, looming over him.

"Hurt Bza, fight me!" rumbled the troll.

"Thorolf!" said Berthar's voice. "I cannot have you treating a high-born lady thus!"

Thorolf rose. "If you're fain to keep those two termagants from killing each other," he snarled, "I wish you joy of the task. I am more concerned with my belly. Chief Wok, who has a bite to spare a hungry fellow tribesman?"

As the day died, Thorolf pitched his little tent at the edge of the village and pulled off his boots. Berthar asked:

"What do ye, Thorolf?"

"As any fool can see, I am stalking a Pantorozian tiger," snapped Thorolf.

"Oh, come, be not angry! Ye were right to separate those twain even if compelled to be rough with them. Are ye going to sleep?"

"Aye. Having been on the dodge for a sennight, I weary."

"Ye take not your usual tent, with Bza?"

"She threatened to cut off my manhood whilst I slept, so I shall rest better alone."

"Then what of the Countess and me? My sack is not spacious enough for two. . . ."

"Ask Wok to find spaces for the twain of you. Yvette was right; this shelter is really not large enough for more than one. Good night."

Later, finding sleep elusive despite his fatigue, Thorolf heard Yvette say:

". . . in Grintz, a commoner who laid violent hands upon me would be torn between wild horses."

"But, my dear, he had to! He did after all save your life."

"So I ween; but it's hard to forgive such presumptuous treatment. My elbow was skinned in the fall, and my arm aches from the twist he gave it."

"Ye should make amends."

"I would have, earlier; but he professed not to hear when I spake. Now he sulks, because I gave him not what . . ."

The voices faded with distance. Thorolf mentally finished her last sentence: ". . . what I gave you." He uttered a little snort of disgust, partly at himself for being, despite all, still in love with the jade.

X
SANGUINARY SWORDS

When Thorolf finally dropped off, he slept heavily, so that the sun was well up before he awoke. As he crawled out and started for the patch of ground on the leeward side of the village used by the trolls for toilet purposes, Chief Wok hailed him:

"Ho there! Know ye what hath become of your Bza?"

"Nay," said Thorolf. "What has?"

"Disappeared, along with young Khop. Methinks they've run off together."

"I'm not surprised. She took Khop as a lover whilst I dwelt with her."

"Oho! Then why haven't ye slain Khop, or at least given him a good drubbing?"

Thorolf grinned at the idea of a human being, even so powerful a one as himself, thrashing the mighty Khop. "I already had my bow trained upon the Countess. My junction with Bza was what we call a marriage of convenience. If she prefer Khop, I shall send good wishes after them.''

Wok shook his head. ''Ye lowlanders are strange beings. Ye are plainly no coward; and yet. . . .''

''Any notion of whither they've gone?''

''Belike to the Dorblentzes to join Chief Yig's horde.''

''Perchance Khop can arrange peace betwixt the hordes. You trolls need all your combined strength to resist lowland encroachments.''

''Me, friends with that louse! . . . But it could be that ye have an idea there, Thorolf. I'll think upon it. Now what of the twain ye brought hither? I found places for them—the woman in mine own tent, though I had to toss out one of my wives.''

Thorolf: ''They won't be here long.'' He looked around and sighted Berthar and Yvette, sitting in a circle of trolls and making the best of a breakfast of smoked goat's meat and barley porridge. They looked up as he approached.

''Heigh-ho, Thorolf!'' said the Countess. ''When canst arrange my safe return to Zurshnitt?''

Berthar said: ''I must spend a day or two seeking my salamanders ere returning to the city.''

''Zurshnitt won't be safe until we've drawn Parthenius' fangs,'' said Thorolf. ''I shall have to get in touch with my father—''

''Nonsense, Thorolf!'' snapped Yvette. ''A man as able as you can surely cleanse that nest of vipers without going through your tedious Rhaetian legalisms!''

''I thank you for the compliment,'' said Thorolf, ''but I fear you overstate mine abilities. I'm no demigod, like that fellow Zorius in your Dualistic religion—the one they sacrificed. What's your True Faith, by the way?''

She shrugged. ''I bend to local beliefs and prejudices, having no fanatical faith of mine own. But why can't you lead the trolls through the tunnels, burst in upon Parthenius and his creatures, and slaughter the lot? If Orlandus be dead, they'll have no wizard to ward them with spells.''

"I have broached the idea," said Thorolf. "Wok refused it as too risky."

"But that was ere Orlandus' death, was't not? Now you'd have a better chance of striking quickly."

"Much depends," Thorolf explained, "on my father's persuading the Senate to recognize the trolls as human."

"But that might take months, whilst your politicians trade favors and strike deals! I'll not endure to be mewed up here amongst these stinking ape-men—"

"Watch your tongue!" Thorolf snapped in Helladic, the international language of scholars. "Some understand you."

"I care not! I gat no sleep last night, jammed in with a lot of trolls, snoring and stinking, and betimes old Wok awakening to futter one or another of's wives, whilst the rest looked on and made ribald comments— I suppose on his performance, if I could have understood their hoggish speech. He asked me if I expected the same service and seemed relieved when I did assure him that I did not. He explained that he was willing to tup me as a matter of simple hospitality, albeit he found me repulsive." She gave a little sputter of laughter. "But you can perceive why life in troll-land has for me no allure."

"Oh, come, Countess," said Berthar soothingly. "We shall get better sleeping arrangements. Whilst we be in exile here, ye can help me to search for my salamanders—"

"Oh, bugger your little lizards!" cried Yvette. "I'll not abide such treatment—"

"My dear," said Berthar with a pained expression, "I have explained that they be not lizards—"

"But I will *not* be cooped and confined—"

"Sorry, your Highness," said Thorolf, "but I know not what else you can do."

He started to walk away. Then something soft and moist struck him smartly in the back of his head. As he spun around, he clapped a hand to the spot. His hand came away with a flattened gob of barley porridge.

Yvette, still seated beside Berthar, dug her spoon into the porridge bowl. She held up the spoon, grasping the stem with the thumb and two fingers of her right hand while with those of her left she pulled back the bowl of the spoon, so that it acted like the throwing arm of a one-armed catapult. Furious, Thorolf shouted:

"If you do that again, I'll spank your pretty pink arse!"

"You wouldn't dare!" she cried, raising the spoon to take aim.

"Try me!" barked Thorolf.

"My lady!" said Berthar, grasping her arm. "I beg you! We dare not fall out; we must stand together—"

He broke off as a troll rushed into the village, shouting: "Foe! Foe! Foe!"

"To arms!" roared Wok. The village burst into frantic motion. Females snatched up their cubs. Males dove for their tents, to emerge with weapons. All yelled at the tops of their powerful voices until the noise was deafening.

Berthar and Yvette sprang up, the latter crying: "Where? Whence come they?"

Shading his eyes, Thorolf peered about until he saw a flash of the sun on armor, along the trail to Zurshnitt. "Yonder!" he cried. "I'll get my crossbow."

Wok hurried the trolls into a ragged line athwart the path of the oncoming force. As the figures grew larger, Thorolf saw that in their van marched three ogres, each half again as tall as a man and bearing a huge club. Behind them came Parthenius, in helmet and half-armor of plate. After him strode a score or so of chain-clad guards from Castle Zurshnitt in Sophonomy's sky-blue surcoats. To Yvette and Berthar, Thorolf growled:

"We need not seek out Parthenius and his merry men; they come to us."

Thorolf felt a tug on his clothing and realized that his dagger was being drawn from its sheath. He turned to see Yvette secreting the weapon in the cloak she had taken from the renegade Carinthian.

"Yvette!" he exclaimed. "What dost? Mean you to stab me?"

"Nay, Thorolf dear. I shall need it in case that swine again lays hands on me."

Beside Parthenius came another figure who, being small, Thorolf did not at once recognize. This turned out to be the fat little treasurer of the Magicians' Guild, Avain.

Real ogres, Thorolf knew, could mash flat ten times their number of human beings, or even trolls. But he had suspicions of these. By looking hard, he could see the twinkle of the sun on the guardsmen's armor through the ogres' scaly bodies; Bardi's spell had not worn off. He turned to Wok, saying:

"Chief, those ogres are mere illusions, cast by—"

At that instant, Wok shouted: "Sorcery! Flee!"

"Wait!" cried Thorolf. But as one troll, the horde turned and ran, bounding up the slope above the village. In a trice Thorolf found himself standing with Berthar and Yvette alone, facing the oncomers. The Sophonomist guards bore swords, pikes, halberds, and bows. When the ogres loomed over the trio, Parthenius cried:

"Halt! Sergeant Thorolf and Countess Yvette, I want you twain; the beast-keeper I care not about. Will ye yield quietly? 'Tis useless to resist; if ye essay to flee, as did the trolls, my archers will bring you down."

"What does Doctor Avain in your ranks?" shouted Thorolf.

"He is our new Psychomagus. Do ye yield?"

Rage had been building up in Thorolf. It seemed to him that, no matter what he did, the Sophonomists were always thwarting him in one way or another. Now, although cooler reflection might have indicated some other course, he whipped the crossbow to his shoulder. The bow thumped; the bolt whistled through one of the illusory ogres and buried itself in the midriff of Avain, whom Thorolf judged to be his most dangerous single foe. With a shriek, the little magician doubled over and sank down. The three ogres vanished.

Thorolf snatched another bolt from its case and stooped to put his foot in the stirrup to recock the weapon, hoping for a shot at Parthenius. Before he could complete the task, the flat of a halberd caught him on the side of his head and knocked him sprawling. He sat up, shaking the stars out of his vision. Two of Parthenius' crew had laid hands on Yvette, despite her struggles, and two more had seized Berthar.

As Thorolf rose, still groggy, guards tried to lay hands on him likewise. He knocked one down and grabbed for his sword, but others clutched at him from all sides. His struggles sent them staggering back and forth, but they hung on. Parthenius stood before him, grinning. The man took off his helmet, exposing a mass of coppery curls.

"I had thought ye'd make a prime diaphane," grated Parthenius, "wherefore I told my men to take you alive. But ye've slain our new magus as well as the old. To keep you captive until we find another were too risky, knowing what a mighty and self-willed wight ye be. The Countess were easier to handle." He turned to a halberdier. "Off with his head!"

The guards holding Thorolf tried to bend him down to afford a fair target for the ax blade, but Thorolf continued to struggle. Parthenius said:

"Come now, Sergeant, wouldn't ye prefer a quick, clean chop to being slowly whittled to death with knives? If ye persist in your contimacy, the latter fate shall be yours.''

"Futter you!" snarled Thorolf.

"Ho!" shouted a guard. "Look yonder!"

The trail from Zurshnitt skirted the village and continued along the mountainside. Along the trail, from the direction opposite the city, came another troop of armed men, about equal to that led by Parthenius. At the head of the column rode a man on a huge white horse. He bore a lance with a flag near its tip, displaying the red boar on a white ground of the Duchy of Landai.

"Form double line!" shouted Parthenius. "Archers on the flanks! Do not let go of the prisoners!"

The mounted man, also in plate, halted his horse and turned his head to shout, in the accents of Carinthia: "Deploy right and left!" He handed his lance to one man, dismounted, and gave his reins to another.

The column split, half the men filing to the right and half to the left, until they formed another double rank facing the Sophonomists. The man in plate stepped forward and, like Parthenius, removed his helmet. He showed a head of graying blond hair with an expanse of pink bare scalp rising through it like a mountaintop above the clouds. Below it were a pair of bulging blue eyes and a large red blob of a nose. While his chin was shaven, he wore a huge mustache, curled at the ends like the horns of a buffalo. He addressed Parthenius:

"Sirrah, who are ye who holds my affianced bride? Release her forthwith, or ye shall die the death!"

"I," said the other, "am the Reverend Doctor Parthenius, Prophet-in-Chief of the mighty Church of Sophonomy. As for the woman, she was happily rising in the ranks of my church when this miscreant—" he indicated Thorolf "—snatched her away. I have rescued her. And who in the seven hells be ye, to question me?"

The blond man gave the ghost of a nod. "Gondomar,

Fifth Duke of Landai, at your service. Release the woman at once!''

"I will not. She is under the evil influence of this soldier and must be brought back into the light of the true spiritual science!''

"I shall count three,'' said Gondomar, "and if by that time those three under distraint be not released, ye and all your men shall die!'' He turned his head and bellowed: "Prepare to charge!''

"One step toward us, and the woman's throat shall be cut!'' yelled Parthenius, seizing Yvette and pinioning her arms.

"Harm one hair of her head, and ye shall die—but slowly!'' replied the Duke.

"Ready to receive the enemy!'' Parthenius called out to his troop. Both lines bristled with weapons.

"Listen to me!'' came Yvette's high voice. "Why should all you brave warriors perish in a fribbling quarrel over me betwixt those two bravos? Let those twain settle it by single combat!''

"What? Ridiculous!'' roared the Duke.

"Absurd!'' echoed Parthenius.

"A daft idea!'' said Gondomar.

"A childish notion!'' said Parthenius.

"Why not try it, your Grace?'' said one of Gondomar's officers. "Ye are a mighty battler.''

" 'Twere a splendid sight!'' said one of Parthenius' warriors. "Go ahead, Master; take him up on it! Ye'll trounce him soundly!''

" 'Tis a fair contest, since ye be well-matched!'' added a Landaian.

Both the Duke and Parthenius were pushed forward, vehemently protesting, by groups of their men. Then the men fell back, leaving the two leaders facing each other a couple of yards apart.

The Duke put on his helmet and buckled the chin strap. "Never hath it been said that a Landai quailed!'' he growled. "Art ready?''

"Aye forsooth!" said Parthenius, adjusting his helmet and drawing his sword. "Have at you!"

The swords met with a clang. Back and forth they went, swords scraping and banging. Now and then came the duller sound of a sword striking armor. Round and round they staggered. The shiny armor became dented and scratched. A few scarlet trickles told where the blades had penetrated the plate. On and on went the fight.

A Carinthian called out: "Ten marks on the Duke!"

"Taken!" cried one of Parthenius' guards.

Unable to inflict a mortal wound, the two grasped their swords in both hands and hewed at each other. As they tired, the fighting came in fits and starts. Between times they leaned on their swords, glared at each other, and drew breath in gasping pants.

At the beginning of one of these pauses, Parthenius stepped back and lowered his blade. Quickly as a viper's strike, Gondomar lunged and drove his point beneath the bars of Parthenius' helmet into the flesh below his jaw and up into the skull. Parthenius reeled back and fell with a clang.

Gondomar stepped back and took off his helmet. One of his men handed him a piece of cloth to wipe his face, covered with sweat despite the coolness.

"So much for that lozel!" he said. "Now, who are these ye hold pinioned? The lady I know; but the other twain?"

Berthar and Thorolf identified themselves.

"Oho!" said the Duke. "So ye are the terrible Sergeant Thorolf, who hath caused such scathe to the men I sent to fetch my affianced bride! What do ye here with her?"

"Sergeant Thorolf," began Yvette, "has rescued me—"

"Please, Yvette, let me talk!" swore Thorolf; but the Countess rushed on:

"—rescued me from your bravos, once on the way to Zurshnitt and again in the city; and then from the castle of this villain lying dead."

"Hath this fellow been intimate with you?" barked Gondomar, pointing at Thorolf.

"That's no affair of yours!"

"Oho, so he hath indeed! We'll soon put him beyond such temptations for ay!"

The Duke started toward Thorolf, who stood with the Sophonomist guards who had seized him but who had released their grip with the fall of their leader. In the rush of events, nobody had thought to disarm Thorolf, who now drew his sword.

"Oho, so the baseborn thinks he can fight!" said Gondomar, pulling on his helmet. "We shall soon see!"

He bored in upon Thorolf, who parried the Duke's angry thrusts and swings. Thorolf knew that, the Duke being armored and he not, there was little chance of defeating his opponent save by a stroke of luck. If the Duke had been a tyro, or if he were exhausted from his previous fight, Thorolf might have had a reasonable chance. But the Duke was a seasoned warrior and had recovered his second wind.

"Unfair!" cried Yvette. "He wants armor!"

"This is no duel but an execution," growled the Duke, whirling his sword in circles and figure-eights.

"We have never fornicated!" cried Yvette. "He's under some silly vow of chastity!"

The Duke paid no attention. Round and round they went, with Thorolf ever backing away. If by defense he could wear down the Duke, there was just a chance. . . .

"Stop them, somebody!" shrilled Yvette. None heeded.

A slash from Gondomar opened a slit in Thorolf's breeches and inflicted a shallow cut on the thigh beneath. Blood began to soak the cloth in a widening stain. The cut stung but did not handicap the sergeant.

Gondomar growled as he fought: "I'll have you impaled, knave! . . . . Ye shall be flayed and rolled in salt. . . . I'll bind your feet to a tree and your hands to my horse, and spur the beast. . . . I'll roast you for a day and a night over a slow fire. . . . I'll cut off your members, little by little. . . ."

Thorolf saved his breath for fighting. A thrust from Gondomar scratched the shoulder of Thorolf through his jacket. A return thrust from Thorolf skittered off the Duke's battered armor.

Gondomar wound up one of his fierce two-handed cuts. As he stepped forward, a flash of motion behind the Duke caught Thorolf's eye; something metallic fluttered through the air. Thorolf could not heed it, being busy parrying the Duke's slash so that the blades met at a shallow angle.

Then the Duke gave an angry grunt. His left leg folded beneath him, so that he went down on one knee. To steady himself, he took his left hand off his hilt and pressed that hand against the ground.

Instantly Thorolf lunged and brought his blade in a slash against the back of Gondomar's gauntleted sword hand. The Duke dropped his sword and shook the bruised hand. Thorolf put a foot on the Duke's sword, seized the crest of Gondomar's helmet with his free hand, and inserted his point through the bars in front of the helmet, a finger's breadth from Gondomar's prominent right eye.

"Yield!" commanded Thorolf.

The Duke looked steadily at him and at the sword blade. His eyes swiveled right and left to the clustered crowd of warriors. At last he said:

"I yield. What would ye? Ransom?"

"I'll tell you. First, command your men to march back to Landai forthwith, and yarely!"

"So ye can slay me at leisure?"

"Not if you follow orders. Go on, command them!"

Duke Gondomar sighed. "Very well. Men! Hear ye me? Ye shall return to the duchy forthwith."

"But, your Grace—" began the officer who had urged the duel with Parthenius.

"Hold thy tongue, and obey!" yelled the Duke. "Wouldst slay me with your havering? Go!"

The crowd of Landaians trickled back along the trail by which they had come. Gondomar shouted after them: "Be sure my horse gets back with you, hale and flush!"

When all were out of sight, Thorolf called: "Berthar! Tie me the Duke's wrists behind his back!"

"What with?" said Berthar.

"Here!" Thorolf held out the strips of cloth that he had used on Yvette. When Gondomar's arms were securely bound, Thorolf said:

"Stand up, your Grace; let's see what ails your leg."

Thorolf discovered his dagger embedded in the muscle of Gondomar's unarmored calf, just above the boot. The Duke's movement dislodged the blade, which fell in the dirt.

"Good gods, Yvette," Thorolf said, "I knew not you were a knife thrower!"

"I have skills you wot not of," she said. "What shall we do with this lump of a Duke?"

"He must be haled to Zurshnitt to stand trial!" said Berthar. "Armed invasion, threats to Rhaetian citizens, duelling, attempted homicide. . . ."

"Oh, bugger your legalisms!" said Yvette. " 'Twere best simply to cut his throat!"

"Dearest!" cried Gondomar. "I did but come for love of you!"

"Nay!" said Thorolf. "I promised—"

"But I did not!" said Yvette, reaching for the knife she had thrown.

"Stop her, Berthar!" said Thorolf. As the Director seized Yvette from behind, Thorolf continued: "See what a lucky escape you had, your Grace?" Then to Berthar and Yvette: "He's a valuable property. The

Commonwealth can get some splendid reparations from this fellow in return for's liberty.''

Yvette swore: ''You're so damnably practical! Not a trace of romance!''

Thorolf ignored the statement. ''Bind up his leg, Berthar; his wound is not grave. Then you might take care of mine.'' He turned to the Sophonomist guards. ''What of you fellows? Your employers are dead, and your so-called Church is about to follow them into oblivion. What will you do for a living?''

An officer said: ''Well, sir, we hadn't thought yet. Hast any ideas?''

''Aye, I have. Our regular army is short of men. If you'll return to Zurshnitt with me, I'll put in a good word for you at the barracks.''

Days later, Thorolf dismounted from his mare and entered the Green Dragon, shaking snow from his cloak and stamping it from his boots. He wore his best civilian suit of scarlet doublet and azure breeches; his hair and beard were newly trimmed.

He found the Countess Yvette in the common room, gorgeous in a new emerald gown and holding court to a circle of adherents who had followed her into exile. She introduced Thorolf around:

''Sergeant, behold my loyal subjects: Sir Maximin, Coppersmith Clodomir, Tanner Gundobald, Attorney Siagro, Merchant Ursus, Captain Magnovald, Freeholder Cautinus. . . .''

She turned back to the group. ''That is all for today, good people. I shall see you a sennight hence, when you shall tell me of your progress in raising loans and enlisting others in our righteous cause. Good night!''

When the followers had departed, Thorolf said: ''How goes the government in exile?''

''Not so well as I should like, but better than I feared. My partisans pay my maintenance here. What of the Sophonomists?''

"Gone with the flowers of autumn. Parthenius had told the diaphanes to stay in the castle, knowing they'd soon be slaughtered in any fight. When he died, they wandered off; I ween their deltas have abandoned them, freeing them to return to normal lives. Orlandus' other officers have fled. When Lodar sent a squad of constables to the castle, they found no one within save a handful of gray-clad probationers who, refusing to believe that the cult was destroyed, continued their sweeping or polishing or whatever other duty their Masters had laid upon them."

"Couldst try to recover that golden gown they gave me?"

Thorolf shrugged. "I'll do what I can; I have filed a claim for the money we gave Orlandus to change you back to a woman. But others have also filed claims, and they speak of auctioning off abandoned property in the castle. So count no unhatched fowls."

She sighed. "A pity; in it I truly looked my rank. But what of you?"

"Not altogether well. Berthar failed of election to his Board; so my academic career seems as far off as ever."

"Why did Berthar fail?"

"For a fribbling reason. A member of the Board, Banker Gallus, sent his old horse to the park with a request that it be given a home for its final years. Berthar, who's a stickler for rules, told the fellow he'd do so if Gallus would furnish a stipend to cover the animal's food and care. The Board member refused, Berthar sent back the horse, and Gallus blackballed Berthar at the next meeting. This despite that she-dragon I captured for them! It confirms Doctor Vipsanio's philosophy of Chaoticism."

"Poor Berthar! Such a pleasant man, too. What of Duke Gondomar?"

"The Supreme Council got him to agree to a ten-thousand-mark reparation and a new commercial treaty. Some lawyers sniffed 'twas unconstitutional to let him go without trial, but the government overbore them. They're holding him till the money arrives. How much to heart his popeyed Grace will take the treaty, since it was extorted by duress, remains to be seen.''

"How did he track us to the trollish village?"

Thorolf grinned. "I wondered, too. So I bought a keg of our best Rhaetian ale and had it borne to the cell where he waits. As cells go, it's comfortable. When I proposed that he and I have a beer guzzle, he huffed and puffed a bit, blowing his mustache out like a window curtain and popping his eyes at me like one of Berthar's snails. But at last he came round. I pointed out that, whereas we were foes in the last affray, we might be allies in the next.

"When he'd drunk enough to float a skiff, he told me. He was lurking in a secret camp when one of that trio who robbed Berthar straggled in and reported. Thereupon Gondomar set out with his company to seek our trail. They got lost or they'd have found us sooner. The uproar the trolls made when the Sophonomists approached revealed the direction they sought. At the end, he and I were singing drunken songs together, and he offered me a post in his forces.''

"What wilt? Take up's offer?"

Thorolf shook his head. "I thought about it; I could do worse. But I'll apply for a permanent sergeancy here, unless I decide to go to Tyrrhenia as a mercenary.''

"Why do that?"

"The Duke of Aemilia is raising a force for war with the Republic of Brandesco. He offers over twice what I'm now paid, and more than I should get from Gondomar. With care, a year with the Aemilians should save me enough to see me through my doctorate.'' Thorolf paused. "Yvette, I love you. If you'll wed me, I will stay and make do on my present pay.''

She turned to him. "Dear Thorolf! Forsooth, I love you, too, after a sort. But I will marry none not of noble blood, nor one so prosaically practical as a

Rhaetian.'' Watching Thorolf's face fall, she continued: "I confess I owe you for all you've done, and honor demands repayment. You are a true hero in your stolid way.''

"Just luck, my dear, as when Orlandus obligingly fell out the window, or Regin warned me of the Sophono-mists' plot, or you pinked Gondomar in the leg. But—ah. . . .''

"If you mean money, all the funds I can raise are bespoken for recovery of my country.''

Thorolf snorted. "I would not take money! Really, Yvette, I may be a Rhaetian, but I'm not so crassly commercial as all that!''

"Well, then, I could give you the pleasure of my body for the night—or even several nights, until I depart for Grintz.''

Thorolf shook his head. "Your offer mightily tempts me, but that's not what I seek. I'm thirty, and it is time I were properly matched. We call it 'settling down.' ''

She flared up. "You have the insolence to reject *me*?''

"My apologies, your Highness.''

"Eunuch! Androgyne! Capon!'' She calmed herself. "I'm sorry; I suppose you have some priggish Rhaetian reason. What were the harm?''

"None whatever, save that I should then become your slave, unable to leave your side to pursue my academic career. I am not cut out for a lady's fancy man.''

"So, it's well and good for me to become *your* slave, which is all a Rhaetian housewife is? You know I'm abler than most men!''

Thorolf shrugged. "So we have an impasse, like one of those paradoxes professors tell of, with no true, just, and sensible answer. Hence I'm off to Tyrrhenia. Belike I shall meet one of that gang who slew my friend Bardi and use him as he deserves.''

"If only you had a drop of noble blood and weren't so damnably Rhaetian!''

Thorolf rose, saying:

181

"My lady may yearn
    For adventures archaic,
And suitors all spurn
    As ignoble or laic,
But she'll never discern
    One who's not too prosaic!"

"That's my problem!" she snapped.

"Good night, my dear!" He rose, picked up his cloak, threw it around him, and strode for the door. Did he or did he not hear behind him a faint whisper of: *"Oh, Thorolf!"*? Whether it was real or only imagined, he kept resolutely on out the door and into the snow.

XI
A Sufficiency of Slaughter

The Plain of Formi, a checkerboard of green and brown fields, stretched away to the range of hills that rose against the blue spring sky. The brown was that of lately plowed earth; the green that of newly sprouted crops. Across the plain the army of Ganeozzi, Duke of Aemilia, advanced in three phalanges of a battalion each.

Each phalanx was a hollow square of pikemen, twenty men on a side and, when up to full strength, three hundred soldiers plus officers. The officers marched inside the square along with drummers, buglers, and adjutants. At each corner of the square marched a formation of crossbowmen. From a safe distance, peasants shouted curses at the damage to their crops.

Each phalanx tramped beneath a forest of pikes, held vertically with little flags on some of the pikes for the subordinate units. The sergeants of each of the four companies in the battalion marched outside the square with halberds over their shoulders. As sergeant of Alpha Company, Thorolf Zigramson tramped in steel cuirass and burganet on the extreme right of the formation, growling:

"Close up there!" "Pick up your feet!" "You're getting out of line!" "Watch the stones lest you trip!" "Sigman, your pike wobbles! Straighten up!"

A quarter-league ahead, the Brandescan Army lay on the rising ground of the saddle between two hills. At that distance it was merely a dark, formless mass, variegated by the banners rising at intervals and sending out little gleams of sun on armor. As the Aemilians neared, Thorolf could begin to make out the forms of individuals. Shouts of command and cheers came faintly across the diminishing distance, mingled with drum beats and bugle calls.

"Battalion, halt!" roared the major from the middle of the square. The underofficers and noncommissioned officers repeated: "Battalion, halt!" Bugle calls and drum beats reinforced the command.

The phalanx stumbled to a halt, with lurching and shoving. Pikes rattled as they struck one another with a clatter like that of storks' bills.

"Dress ranks!" cried the major. This command, too, was repeated. The sergeants bustled about, shouting and shoving to align their men. The colonel trotted by on his horse, followed by several mounted adjutants. He exchanged shouts with the majors commanding the three battalions.

Vulkop, the sergeant of Beta Company, also with halberd on shoulder, wandered around the corner of the phalanx to Thorolf. During a lull, Vulkop said softly: "I like it not, Thorolf." He jerked a thumb toward the Brandescan Army. " 'Tis said the foe have a mort of thunder tubes yonder, of a new and deadlier kind."

"One of those stone balls may strike down a few," said Thorolf, "but we shall be upon them long ere they can reload."

"I hear they shoot, not stones, but balls of iron," persisted Vulkop. "That makes these 'guns,' as they call them, nimbler and farther-reaching. I've warned the officers, but I might as well have bespoken the deaf."

"I, too, have told them we shall need a new plan of battle, to no avail," replied Thorolf. "The push of the pike, quotha, will ever rule the field. And where the devil's our cavalry?"

"Late as usual," snarled Vulkop, trotting back around the corner of the formation.

After an eternity of waiting, while officers conferred and noncoms nagged their men, the major commanded:

"Attention! Front rank, lower pikes!"

The pikes of the first rank came down to horizontal. "Second rank, slant pikes!"

The pikemen behind those in front lowered their pikes to an angle of thirty degrees, holding so that they passed between the heads of the soldiers in front of them.

"Arbalesters, cock your weapons!"

The crossbowmen at the corners each placed the muzzle of his device on the ground and put a foot into the stirrup in the nose. They squatted, seized the bow-string in both hands, and bent the bow as they straightened up with a grunt and a heave.

"Prepare to charge!"

Thorolf pushed his way between the men to the inner side of the square. His rôle was to continue to command and discipline the men from the inner side. If the enemy threatened to break into the square, he would stiffen the resistance with swings of his halberd.

Shouts arose from the phalanx. Out from the ends of the Brandescan line streamed squadrons of cavalry. As they neared, Thorolf saw from their baggy garments and turbans that they were Saracens, brandishing scimitars, javelins, and bows. He had heard that Brandesco, weak in cavalry, had hired these foreign horsemen to

185

make up the lack. Yelling, the Saracens galloped toward the Aemilian phalanxes.

"Hedgehog!" screamed the major. "Hedgehog! Hedgehog!" came the shouts of his subordinates.

The outermost ranks and files of the phalangites faced outward, knelt, and jammed the butts of their pikes into the soft earth. Behind them, the second ranks slanted their pikes as the second rank of the front had done before, thus presenting a spiky obstacle all the way round the formation.

The arbalesters at the corners discharged their crossbows with a rattle of thuds. Although they could hardly miss at that range, they did no visible harm.

Along the Brandescan line, puffs of smoke bloomed to cauliflower shape. Half a heartbeat later came the crash of cannon fire. Cannon balls sailed overhead or plowed up the soft earth on either side. The men of the battalion set up a jeering outcry:

"Couldn't hit the side of a mountain!"

"Attention!" came the command. Again the pikes were raised to vertical, while the kneeling soldiers rose. Delay followed as officers conferred and sergeants cursed their men to get them lined up. The colonel and his adjutants galloped past, throwing up clods of mud. At last came the command:

"Prepare to charge!"

Along the Brandescan line in the nearer distance, Thorolf glimpsed men rushing about, swabbing out gun barrels and hefting iron balls and bags of powder.

"Charge!" yelled the major. "Charge! Charge!" cried the others.

The phalanx started forward at a trot. As the Brandescan line came closer, the Saracens hovering out of crossbow range swept in again, whooping and yelling.

"Halt! Hedgehog!"

The men obeyed, more raggedly than the first time. Then the Brandescan cannon opened up again. Two balls plowed into Thorolf's phalanx, with a crash that mingled the crackle of shattering spears with the din of breaking men in armor. Pikes toppled; screams arose.

"Close up! Close up!" bellowed the sergeants.

"Attention! Prepare to charge! Charge!" came the commands.

Again the formation started forward, leaving the wounded and slain sprawled on the brown earth. Again came the Saracen charge, the hedgehog, and the cannon volley. Several cannon balls plowed into the formation; more pikes toppled. In addition, a crackle of handgun fire ran down the Brandescan line. Commands were drowned out by a rising chorus of screams and yells from the wounded. Sergeant Vulkop shouted in Thorolf's ear:

"Another volley like that and we shall be down to half our strength! The men are wavering!"

"Where's the major?"

"There he is, what's left!" Vulkop pointed to a headless body in half-armor, lying with several others within the square. All the officers had fallen or disappeared.

The Saracens whirled past as the crossbowmen got their weapons cocked and let fly. Thorolf stumbled over a mess of spilled entrails. He told his two surviving fellow sergeants:

"There's something feigned about those Saracens. They shoot their arrows or cast their darts not; and our arbalesters' bolts go through them and their horses without harm."

"Sorcery!" said Sergeant Herminus.

"Aye; the Saracens are but an illusion cast by their wizards, to halt us in range of their tubes. If we can get the men moving again, one good charge, ignoring the illusions—"

"Too late!" said Vulkop. "Look yonder!" He pointed to the middle one of the three phalanxes. It was breaking up; men were leaving their shattered ranks and streaming back across the plain. Most of them dropped their pikes to move faster.

"And yonder!" said Herminus, pointing toward the

Brandescan line, from the ends of which rode more cavalry. These were no phantom Saracens but armored lancers bearing the eagle flag of Brandesco on their lance tips.

Thorolf, tripping over a severed leg, hurried around the square, bellowing: "Get back in line! Get in line! Hold your posts, if you would not be stuck like pigs! It's your only chance!" Where a couple of men dropped their pikes and started off as the men of the other phalanxes were doing, he pushed through to the outside and drove the men back into ranks with blows of the shaft of his halberd.

By shouting himself hoarse and by blows and kicks, with the help of the other sergeants he got the surviving men back into a ragged hedgehog formation. A squadron of Brandescan lancers rode up, then sheered off from the hedge of pikes and galloped away across the plain after easier targets, the backs of the fleeing phalangites. Then the Aemilian cavalry, long overdue, appeared; but at the sight of the two broken phalanxes they turned about and rode off, leaving the Brandescan riders to spear the fleeing foot until the plain was carpeted with bodies.

Thorolf's surviving phalanx tramped its way in a stolid square back across the plain, presenting a ready hedgehog of pikes every time a group of Brandescans came nigh. The walking wounded limped along inside the square. The more seriously stricken had perforce to be left to the mercy of the Brandescans.

Without planning to do so, Thorolf had fallen into command of his group by energy, brawn, and presence of mind. The other sergeants seemed willing to follow his lead.

Night had fallen when the group, down to fewer then two hundred, reached the village of Formi.

Under a sinking half-moon, Formi seemed curiously deserted; no villagers were in sight. Instead, a few men of the Aemilian army, many staggering drunk, moved about the streets, in which lay several bodies in peasant garb.

As Thorolf's battalion moved into the main street in column of fours, the rabble of soldiers moved aside. Some called out:

"Where in hell did you knaves come from? The battle was lost, was it not?"

"Who are you?" asked Thorolf.

"Never mind who I am. I got away with a whole skin, which most of my comrades did not."

"Where are the villagers?"

"In hell or in hiding. When we slew a few who crossed us, the rest thought a little travel good for their health." The man giggled. "Help yourself to the locals' wine; some is not bad. Otmar of the Third caught a pig the locals were not quick enough in getting away; the lads are roasting it."

"Where's the Duke?"

The soldier shrugged. "None hath seen him since the rout. Belike he galloped back to Fiensi with his gentlemen, to shut the gates against our comrades demanding their pay."

"What befell the wagon train, with our rations?"

"Gone on ahead, with the cavalry."

"Then is there aught to eat here?"

"A few loaves and the like in the houses, if the lads haven't eaten them all."

"Stupid oafs," muttered Sergeant Herminus. "Veterans know what to do with a village. Don't chase the villagers out; command them to stay and to feed and shelter you and allow you a go at their women, on the promise not to burn their town. There's nought like hunger to touch off a mass desertion."

Thorolf and the other sergeants agreed to divide the battalion, each to take his group to a different part of town to seek quarters, and then to reunite at sunrise.

* * *

Thorolf's men at last found a group of houses containing only a couple of fugitive soldiers. The other troopers they tossed out and made do with the few provisions left in the peasants' larders. When a fight threatened over a cabbage, Thorolf grabbed the combatants and banged their heads together until they agreed to an equitable division.

The houses of the more prosperous peasants were two-storey structures, the upper storey being the living quarters and the lower a barn for carts, implements, and livestock. The owners of these three houses had driven away their oxen, goats, and asses when they fled.

Thorolf had taken off his boots and, with two others, had lain down on the main bed when female shrieks came to his ears. Pulling on his boots and seizing his sword, he went out and scrambled down the outside stair to the street. The moon had set, but the feeble light from rooms in which lamps or candles burned enabled him to see his way.

The sounds were coming from the house to the right of that which he and a score of other soldiers occupied. The main room on the second level shed candlelight.

Thorolf mounted the stair of this building, which he had assigned to another score of his soldiers. The door was open, and sound and motion came from within.

Thorolf stepped into the peasant's bed-sittingroom. The soldiers were crowded in the middle and did not notice Thorolf's arrival. He grasped a couple by the slack of their jackets and hauled them away from the ring. One snarled: "How now, thou whoreson—" but fell silent when he recognized Thorolf.

In the middle of the crowd, Thorolf now saw, a woman lay on her back on the floor, with her skirt and petticoat pulled up to her chin and four men holding her down, one on each limb. Her outcries were now muffled by a gag. A fifth man, kneeling upright between her spread legs, had just pulled down his breeches, showing a lusty erection.

Thorolf pushed into the circle, grasped the man by his hair, hauled him erect, and dealt him a buffet that sent him falling backward over another soldier, one of the pair holding the woman's ankles.

"Let her go!" Thorolf roared.

"And who in hell be ye?" began the man holding the other ankle. Thorolf's boot caught him in the ribs and tumbled him over.

The men holding the woman's wrists let go and uncertainly got to their feet. The woman pulled out the gag, put down her skirt, and rose likewise.

"You bastards heard your orders!" said Thorolf. "No beating, robbing, or raping. Do you want the countryside hunting us down? Know you what peasants do to stragglers from a beaten army when they catch them? Skin them alive! The next offender shall be hanged—"

A fierce blow with a blade caught Thorolf on the side of the face. The blow staggered him, but he recovered his balance and whirled. The would-be rapist had pulled up his breeches, taken up a sword, and come at Thorolf from behind.

"That for thee, misbegotten swine!" shouted the man.

To escape another slash, Thorolf sprang back, bowling over another trooper. Before the swordsman could close to finish him, Thorolf got his sword out. The blades clanged. Everyone yelled:

"Clear a space! Clear a space!" "That was a foul blow!" "Stop them, somebody!" "Why stop a good fight?" "Tenpence on the sergeant!" "I'll take Frinzl if ye'll give me odds!"

Back and forth, round and round went Sergeant Thorolf and Pikeman Frinzl, hacking and thrusting. At last Thorolf got a thrust home on Frinzl's arm. As the wounded arm sagged, Thorolf sent a full-armed lunge into Frinzl's chest. Frinzl, like nearly all the other surviving men of the First Battalion, had arrived in Formi wearing either a cuirass or a mailshirt over an acton;

but Frinzl's defenses were piled in a corner of the room with others. Frinzl staggered back, coughed blood, and sagged to the floor.

"Anyone else?" said Thorolf to the suddenly quiet crowd, holding his sword with a drop of blood forming on the point. He knew that all they needed was a vigorous leader to rouse them against him, and he would be pulled down and slain in a trice, like a stag by hounds or wolves. They would be furious at his spoiling their gang rape; but no leader spoke up.

"Then throw this carrion into the street, and the lot of you get out!" he continued, speaking with difficulty because of the gaping wound on his face.

The men shuffled out the door and down the stairs, two bearing the late Trooper Frinzl. Thorolf heard a mutter: "Damned bluenosed Zurshnitters hate to see anyone else having fun. . . ."

Thorolf turned to the woman, who shrank back. Now that he had a chance to view her more closely, she was young, quite comely, and just a trifle plump.

"How came they to catch you?" he asked in Tyrrhenian.

"I pray you, sir, I had lain down for a nap when the soldiers came. My parents fled with my brothers and sisters in such haste that they forgot to awaken me."

"How could your parents forget one of their own children?"

"I am the eldest of eight; so I ween they lost count. And now what, sir? Am I to be raped by you alone instead of by the whole battalion?"

"You shan't be raped at all, if I can prevent."

"Oh, thank you, sir. Meanst it that ye have lost your member in the wars?"

Thorolf gave a laugh that was half a gurgle because of the blood in his mouth. "Nay indeed. But this cut on my face begins to hurt abominably. Canst wash it and show me what it looks like?"

"Oh, yea, sir. Sit ye down here, and I'll wash it and sew it up."

She brought in a bronze mirror, which gave a wobbly image of Thorolf with a huge gash on his right cheek, through which some of his teeth could be glimpsed. Below it his face and garments were soaked with blood.

"This will hurt," she said.

"Go ahead," said Thorolf. "A soldier must expect such dolors. Ouch!"

While the stitching and the pains associated with it took nearly all of Thorolf's attention, he became aware that the young woman was silently weeping. When the last bit of thread had been tied, he took his mind off the ache long enough to say:

"Why weep you—and what is your name, by the way?"

"Ramola, sir."

"Very well, Ramola, why weep you? Your family seem to have gotten clean away, and you've been rescued from a gang rape."

The tears trickled silently. "I do think on what will befall me, for now I shall never get a decent husband."

"How so?"

"No local swain will ever believe I was not futtered by the soldiers; and they are fussy about virgin brides, notwithstanding that they all go to the city to tup the whores. I see nought ahead but a short life of city whoredom."

"You want a husband, then?"

"Oh, certes, good sir. In Aemilia, a woman's nought without one."

Thorolf remained silent for a space, dabbing at his cheek with a cloth Ramola had given him. At last he said: "In good sooth, it happens that I need a wife. Would the post beguile you?"

"Why, sir, I never thought of wedding a foreigner. But in view of your acture tonight, ye cannot be all evil, even if a foreigner and a soldier. Suffer me to think on the matter. Think ye we should come to love each other, as do the luckiest couples?"

"Belike. There is but one way to find out."

"Whilst I think on the matter, that dried blood on your garments doth begin to stink. Let me wash them!"

A year after his departure from Rhaetia, when the last snow of spring was melting and dripping from eaves, Captain Thorolf Zigramson knocked on the door of Director Berthar's chamber of office in the Zoölogical Park. When he entered, Berthar leaped up, crying:

"Thorolf! I feared you dead! What hath befallen? I see ye have a new scar."

Thorolf touched his right cheek, where the ridged purple-and-white scar showed above the edge of his beard. "No great matter; I lost no teeth, albeit I was bedded for a fortnight in the lazaretto at Fiensi by a fever. How about you?"

Berthar grinned. "I made the Board at last. Lust ye still after your professorship?"

"By Kernun's antlers, indeed I do! I've seen enough soldiering for a lifetime."

"What happened? I heard your Duke's forces were routed."

"So they were, and soundly. The Brandescans had a mort of Serican thunder tubes, or 'guns' as they call them nowadays. We were advancing by battalions in phalanx formation . . ." Thorolf narrated the Battle of Formi. "I saw that this Saracen horse were but illusions cast by the Brandescans' wizards; but by then our formations were breaking up."

"I heard ye heroically saved the remnant of your battalion."

Thorolf shrugged. "After our officers had fallen, I saw no way to survive save an orderly retreat, and by shouting and beating with the flat I kept them in ranks and brought them off."

"Bravo! How didst keep your head in the confusion?"

"Simple logic. If a group of men afoot are assailed by horsemen, which gives them the better chance of survival: to present a steady line of pikes, or to flee, presenting their defenseless backs? That's why I am now captain. The Duke offered a colonelcy if I would stay, but I declined.''

''Wherefore?''

''Not how I wish to spend my life.''

''What next, then?'' asked Berthar.

''The regulars will take me back with a captain's rank, now that old Gunthram has retired. I might accept, if I get no academic appointment.''

''Fear not for that post at Horgus!'' cried Berthar. ''Betwixt my advocacy and your war record, it's as certain as the sun's rise. Tetricus is back and will help.''

''Good; but I will rejoice when 'tis in my grasp. And how wags your world?''

''Excellent! My lady dragon hath egged, and all do eagerly await its hatch. My colleagues have accorded the mountain salamander the rank of species, which I have named *Salamandra thorolfi* in requital of your saving me from those bravos.''

Thorolf grinned. '' 'Twill not make me as famous as Arnalt of Thessen; but 'tis earthly immortality of a sort.''

Berthar unhooked a watch the size of his fist from his belt, held it up, and stared at its single hand, while it emitted an audible clank-clank, clank-clank. ''Time to close shop. Wilt dine with us?''

''Gramercy; but where?''

''At my home. I'm wed again.''

''So am I, to a Tyrrhenian lass. We're looking for quarters for us, our expected, and my father, who must vacate the palace for loss of the election.''

''Fetch her along!''

An hour later, Thorolf knocked on the door of Berthar's house, with a stocky, black-haired young woman on his arm. As the door opened, Thorolf suppressed a gasp. Yvette, beautiful as ever, stood in the doorway, clad like a decent bourgeois housewife. Berthar loomed behind her, saying:

"Thrice welcome, Thorolf. You know my wife."

"Ah—yea indeed," said Thorolf, turning to the woman beside him. "Darling, these are Doctor Berthar and his wife, Yvette of Grintz. I present my wife, Ramola of Formi."

"I am honor to know you," said Ramola in slow, heavily accented Rhaetian. "Excuse, please; I no speak you language much yet."

Dinner came, with all four acting circumspectly. Thorolf retold the tale of his campaign: ". . . and the sad thing was that Formi was burned down after all; some drunken soldiers upset a lamp. We heard about it in Fiensi."

Yvette asked: "Didst ever find any of those rascals who slew the old iatromagus?"

"A curious thing, that. A month after the battle, I sat in a mughouse in Parmiglia, when a blind beggar came up, feeling his way with a stick. I gave him a few pence, whereat he asked in a Carinthian accent if he might sit for a spell to rest his feet. Although his face was dreadfully scarred and pitted, there was something familiar about him. With a little prodding he told his tale.

"He'd soldiered for the Brandescans and had been set to mixing the devil-powder for their guns. Something went awry; the stuff exploded in his face and destroyed his sight. He thought 'twas the gods' revenge for having slain an old magician not long before.

"When I asked if the magician was Bardi in Zurshnitt and if his name was Offo, he gave a squawk of terror and made for the door, stumbling in his haste."

"Didst slay him as planned?" she asked.

Thorolf shrugged. "What good? The gods—if in fact 'twas gods and not blind chance—had punished him more cruelly than ever I could. So I finished the wine I'd bought him and let him go, tapping his way and muttering. Who am I to judge the gods' revenges?"

* * *

Afterward, Berthar took Ramola off on a tour of his terraria of frogs and salamanders, lecturing her in fluent Tyrrhenian. Yvette took Thorolf aside, saying:

"I knew nought of this. Art happy?"

"Within reason. And you? What of your country and your blue blood?"

"My expedition to Grintz collapsed like a ruptured bladder. Word came that Gondomar had died in some silly skirmish; the King of Carinthia appointed a new Duke of Landai and a new Count of Grintz. These raised powerful forces to resist my restoration. So my loyal subjects melted away like the snows of spring, and I faced the alternatives of marriage, whoredom, or starvation. Oh, curse it all, if only I were not a woman and a little wisp of one at that! Were I a man with your thews, I'd get my title back, fear not!"

After a pause she continued: "I am sorry for Gondomar in a way. He was not truly a wicked man—dull, pompous, and insistent on his own way, but not vicious like Parthenius. I suppose he did love after his fashion. I've wondered . . ." She paused again.

"So," she resumed, "seeing no hope of resuming my rightful place, and with you away in Tyrrhenia . . ." She spread her hands. "I like Berthar well enough. He's sweet-tempered, kind, and gentle, albeit he spends so much time with his stinking beasts and slimy reptiles that I see but little of him. Moreover, he's nearly old enough to be my sire; so his blood runs not so hotly as mine."

"Meaning he can no longer futter all night every night, eh?"

"Thorolf! Such language to a—but I forget I'm no longer a peeress."

"I've heard blunter from you."

"Yea, but that's the privilege of the nobly born. You commoners should use it only amongst yourselves, never to us of noble blood."

Thorolf smiled. "I'll essay to remember, your Highness. Dost keep Berthar's house?"

She grimaced. "Betimes the cook gets drunk, or the maid departs without warning—torts we'd punish with stripes in Grintz. Canst picture me, descendant of a hundred kings and princes, cooking, making beds, and sweeping? I *hate* it, *hate* it, *hate* it!"

"My condolences. What of your coronet?"

"Waddo Sifson took it as security for's loan. When I couldn't repay, the damned ignoble dreg distrained the thing, with no pity for a lone woman struggling for her birthright. He's selling the coronet to the new Count of Grintz—that whoreson Crannus, who has no more noble blood than a turnip. His mother was once wed to the Baron of Klattern and has named herself 'Baroness' ever since, after the Baron divorced her for infidelity. Crannus is her son by another husband but calls himself 'Lord Crannus' regardless. I hope the coronet crushes his brain."

She gave Thorolf a piercing look and seized his arm in a grip of painful force. "Thorolf! Listen hard! Much as I hate to admit it, I was a fool to reject your proposal, ere you went off soldiering. Let's flee to some far land and start over, you and I! Our mutual passion had been glorious, had fate permitted. 'Tis not too late!"

Smiling, Thorolf shook his head. "Nay, my dear!"

"Why not? It were a wonderful adventure!"

"For one, I've had my fill of adventures. For another, I am well pleased with my little Ramola. If my feeling be not one of white-hot passion, it suits me well."

"A passionate Rhaetian were like a flying tortoise!"

"Besides, she's pregnant; Berthar is a friend; and I try to meet mine obligations."

She sniffed. "At least you've proved you *can*. Betimes I wondered. But with those thews, you are plainly made for a life of lusty action, not burrowing in dusty tomes like a man-shaped bookworm."

"Thank you, but I know my own bent."

"You could take us both to the Saracenic lands, where

bigamy is lawful. Some Saracens are said to be true gentlemen."

"Some are true gentlemen everywhere; the problem is to pick them out of the mass. But what on earth should I do in the Saracen lands?"

"Soldier or teach. You're good at both."

Thoughtfully, Thorolf spoke: "I have no more lust for soldiering; nor could I teach until I had mastered Saracenic. Nay, my dear, to hare off on such a lune, when my life's true ambition is within my grasp, were as foolish as leaping off the Temple of Irpo, hoping to fly by flapping one's arms. So make the best of what you have, as I shall do.

"You know that you and I could never have made a lasting couple. You are of too fiery, mercurial, and autocratic a nature. I should be like the snow man in the fairy tale, who was loved by a fire elemental. So you did us both a favor by dismissing my suit."

"But, Thorolf dearest, do but consider—"

"Nay, I will not argue further. I have decided what I shall do."

She spat an expletive in Carinthian peasant dialect. "You're right, I ween; but you Rhaetians are so damnably practical! You miss so much in life."

Thorolf smiled equably. "Including much I am happy to miss, like having my head taken off by a gun ball, as befell our major."

"You'd never make a hero of romance."

"Not my ambition, luckily. You'd find me insufferably dull. If it vexes you that Berthar neglect you for his birds and beasts, be assured that I should vex you even more by neglecting you for dusty tomes and crumbling manuscripts. Psst! Yvette, wipe your eyes! Here they come. . . . Time to depart, Berthar; and many thanks."

"Good night, Professor!" said Berthar.

About the Authors

L. Sprague de Camp, who has over one hundred books to his credit, writes in several fields: biography, historicals, SF, and popularizations of science. But he is a master of that rare animal, *humorous fantasy*.

In 1976, he received *The Gandalf–Grand Master Award for Lifetime Achievement in the Field of Fantasy*. And The Science Fiction Writers of America presented him with their *Grand Master Nebula Award of 1978*.

Catherine Crook de Camp, Sprague's wife of half a century, personal editor, and business manager, has also collaborated with him on numerous works of science fiction and fantasy. This close and loving couple travel everywhere together and are welcome guests at fan conventions throughout the United States.

The de Camps now live in north-central Texas, where the gentler climate and proximity to their two sons, both distinguished engineers, seem to have stimulated their literary productivity. Among their upcoming works are several novels and Sprague's autobiography *Time and Chance*.

Catherine & Sprague De Camp